The Pulpwood Annie Chronicles

Droll Stories About a South Georgia Hooker
and a Smart-Aleck College Guy

by
Max Courson

PublishAmerica
Baltimore

First printing

ISBN: 1-4137-6699-4
PUBLISHED BY PUBLISHAMERICA, LLLP
www.publishamerica.com
Baltimore

Printed in the United States of America

To daughter Shannon, whose successful fiction writing inspired me to try my hand, also.

To wife Naomi, who held her nose but edited my manuscript, anyway.

To ever-tolerant daughters Melinda and Sharon for their unqualified, encouraging support.

To granddaughter Mary Katherine, who some day will be old enough to read her grandfather's book.

Acknowledgments

Anyone who attempts to write in a humorous vein is likely to be indebted to the entertainment and inspiration provided by other genre writers. Such is the case here.

I tip my hat to—among others—Samuel Clemens, Booth Tarkington, David Ross Locke (a.k.a. Vesuvius Petroleum Nasby), Guy Owen, Robert Benchley, Cornelia Otis Skinner, Vladimir Nabokov, John Kennedy Toole, Erma Bombeck, Lewis Grizzard, Carl Hiaasen and Tim Dorsey. May your tribes increase.

I wish to acknowledge Thomas Bulfinch and his epic work, *Bulfinch's Mythology*, for providing classical stories and characters, several of which were updated and incorporated into Annie's notorious adventures.

I wish to acknowledge Homer's *Iliad* for inspiring certain aspects of Chapter 1.

I wish to acknowledge my late brother, John Hinson Courson, whose adolescent blunders, mishaps and malapropisms inspired much of the material involving the Paulk cousins in Chapter 4.

I wish to acknowledge the late Wayne Ruff for providing information that inspired the episode in Chapter 13.

I wish to acknowledge the late Willie Foster Sellers for providing information that inspired episodes in chapters 14 and 15.

Awards

Chapter 9: Pulpwood Annie and the Bootlegger—honorable mention, Norumbega Short Story award, University of Maine, 2004

Chapter 2: Regarding Pulpwood Annie's Patriotic Gesture—first place, ByLine Magazine's Genre Fiction (Humor), fall 2003

Chapter 1: Being Her Unexpected Trip to Floridy—first place, ByLine Magazine's First Chapter of a Novel Contest, 2003

Chapter 10: Pulpwood Annie and the Diamond Ring—third place, fiction entry, Tampa Writers Alliance 17th Annual Writing Contest, 2003

Table of Contents

Comedia Personae

Pulpwood Annie. A south Georgia hooker with a seemingly endless number of wild stories to tell about herself, her relatives, her friends and her customers.

The smart-aleck college guy. An occasional visitor to the Zenobia, Georgia, hot spots, usually seeking beer, and always encountering Annie.

Gene Talmadge Minyon. Revenge-seeking brother-in-law to Helen, who has taken off to Atlanta with her boyfriend, Faris Trion. Gene wants to get Helen back before her husband sobers up and misses her.

Bubba Sweat. Owner of Bubba's Bar in Zenobia, scene of many encounters between Annie and the smart-aleck college guy.

Archie Carter. Soldier on leave who tells wild tales at Bubba's.

Little Paul Lowe. Pulpwooder with an interest in dead snakes and Annie.

Great-Uncle Charlie. Annie's notorious relative with a universal and continual yen for young women, including his close female relatives.

Daisy Sapp. One of Great-Uncle Charlie's conquests.

Arthur Gus Sapp. Daisy's son.

Wormy Willie. One of Annie's less energetic relatives.

Humbug, Grunt and Rooster Paulk. Star-crossed residents of Zenobia and Annie's occasional, smelly customers.

Pennick Ravi Patel. East Indian owner of the Honeysuckle Motel in Zenobia.

Elwood and Mildred Zablonski. The people who unloaded their undesirable motel on Pennick Ravi Patel.

Pickett Poindexter. Ex-con filling station, funeral parlor and cemetery owner and Annie's occasional customer.

Majul Vishra Patel. East Indian hit man hired to finish off Pickett's ugly wife.

Deanna Mae Poindexter. The ugly wife.

Lulu. The smart-aleck college boy's nubile cousin.

Dennis Eichelberger. Computer salesman and Annie's marathon customer.

Selene Gustafson Eichelberger. Dennis' frigid wife

Hovis and Jervis Crummey. Father and son team working on the SMB & A Railroad and who visit Annie whenever they are in town.

Olga Turnipseed. Rail-thin bride who asks Annie to be in her wedding.

Ramses Jones. Huge, lumbering bridegroom.

A.C. Peacock. Local moonshiner and Annie's occasional customer.

Vera Peacock. A.C.'s vengeful wife.

Evie and Ayers Peacock. A.C. and Vera's children

Hector Bryan. A.C.'s bodyguard.

Indian Lil. Savannah prostitute and friend of Annie's.

Vance Roper. Repellant but wealthy son of the town millionaire.

Sam Roper. The millionaire.

Tiffany Odum. Vance's nearsighted bride.

Dewey Swain. Annie's handsome, loudmouthed lover.

Sister Sophie Summerall. Glamorous local radio preacher and tent revival evangelist.

Old Man Moody. County employee specializing in repairing wooden bridges.

Friendly Freddie. Loutish emcee for a local TV talent show.

Squirrel Johnson. Addled tax collector.

Tizzie and Megan. Whorish daughters of Great-Uncle Charlie.

Alec. Limp-wristed son of Great-Uncle Charlie.

Darlene Faye Stone. One of Annie's sluttish friends who is also a kleptomaniac.

Elmore Tittle. Darlene's Dixie Mafia boyfriend.

Uncle Hiram. Elmore's murderous uncle.

Julius Caesar Mincey. One of Annie's favorite Dixie Mafia boyfriends.

Pussycat Boatright. Another Dixie Mafia type who enjoys Annie's favors.

Rudy Rouse. Slow-thinking, petty crook used by Julius and Pussycat in some of their Dixie Mafia criminal acts.

Donnie Dean. Another dim-witted crook who takes part in Dixie Mafia crimes.

Scar Crapps. Pistol-packing boyfriend whom Annie accompanies on several capers.

Ruby Pearl. Slatternly waitress and trick-turner at Bubba's Bar.

LeRoy. Annie's least favorite customer.

Chapter 1

Being Her Unexpected Trip to Floridy

I was firmly ensconced on my favorite rickety stool at Bubba's Bar, sipping on a Miller. Neon signs promoting a catholic collection of cheap brews glowed and blinked in the Stygian gloom. Squeaky overhead fans reshuffled the virtually visible oxygen and the collective odor of hops, hamburger grease and hair tonic. A crowd of farmers, truck drivers and a scattering of hard-eyed women mingled at the pool tables and shuffled around the dance floor to a mournful Merle Haggard "drankin'" song. I was trying without much success to get into the mood of the moment when a gravelly female voice cut through the atmosphere like a shovel through cow plop.

"Well, well, if it ain't the know-it-all college sprout! Hell, sonny, you got your mother's permission to be suckin' on them suds?"

Of course, it was my latest, if not most memorable, encounter with the predatory/amatory Pulpwood Annie, self-styled queen of the south Georgia truck stop and honky-tonk whores.

"Geez, Annie, who let you out of jail, and how many johns did you drain to make up your bail money?" I replied breezily.

"Up yours! I ain't been in jail! I been down to Floridy! Want me to tell you about it?"

Without waiting for a reply, much less an invitation, Pulpwood Annie hoisted herself onto an adjacent stool, including in the effort her patented spread-legged, see-all-the-way-to-Sunday-morning sprawl that tested both the tensile strength of her miniskirt cloth and the savoir faire of some gaping guzzlers at a nearby pool table. She scratched someplace high on her right thigh, near the tattoo of a rabid-looking rose, rearranged her less-than- voluminous bosom and flashed me her best Two-Bucks-And-I-Am-Yours smile.

For reasons best known to God Almighty, I had become a favorite of Pulpwood Annie's. Maybe it was because she had some kind of feral admiration for anybody who had advanced beyond the eighth grade, which was her high-water mark. However, it probably was because I was the only man south of Macon, west of Augusta, east of Columbus and north of Folkston who hadn't sampled her limited but well-known sexual menu. Since most of her early customers had been yahoos driving trucks loaded with logs for the coastal pulpwood mills, I guess she acquired her working name more or less by osmosis.

Occasionally when I came home for a weekend from the University of Georgia, and lacking access to beer in my normally "dry" home town, I would hop in my car and drive over to Zenobia, an equally small cracker community but with beer, wine and whiskey for sale. Symbiotic developments from this economic and social blessing were the various bars, joints and honky-tonks that sprang up just south of the intersection of U.S. 23 and fabled U.S. 1, the old tourist road that runs like a curly black snake from the Canadian border to Key West. Nailed together with more zest than craftsmanship and adorned with long tubes of garish red and green neon tubes, these dens of "entertainment" offered imaginative and sometimes truly surprising outlets for the mill workers, pulpwooders, undiscriminating tourists and curious novices to manhood who populated their premises. And all were grist for the ever-churning erotic mill of Pulpwood Annie.

A woman of indeterminate age, although well on the wrong side of thirty, Annie boasted the usual south Georgia dishwater blonde hair, squinty eyes and a rather lumpy figure that was not helped by various bruises and tattoos from former boyfriends and rough trade. Her legs were somewhat shapely, although the calves needed a bit more exposure to a feedlot, as they say in Texas.

Annie had a modernist approach to what she wore in that she endorsed the minimalist ideal. It was long before the days of Velcro, and I often wondered if she kept those bits of cloth and string strategically attached to her body with liberal applications of Elmer's Glue. Added to this sometimes malodorous package was Annie's unrelenting insensitivity to propriety. It was widely rumored throughout south Georgia that on the day God was issuing couth, Annie was checking out the Blue Light Special at K-Mart.

Anyway, something within the freckled breast of Pulpwood Annie stirred the first time she laid eyes on me. She walked over, asked me how my hammer was hanging and began cadging me for a beer. I responded with my usual collegiate suavity by gagging on my drink and nearly spewing a mouthful on her dress.

After a somewhat foamy introduction, I agreed to add one more Miller to my tab, and Annie plopped down beside me. The rest is history, especially her unrelenting effort to lure me into her somewhat Technicolored arms. That I managed to resist with some degree of civility—not always!—apparently added to my allure. In time, a sort of truce evolved in which she would flirt and tell me the most outrageous stories involving her or some of her soiled-dove friends, and I would somehow evade the inevitable invitation for a tryst. To be honest, my usual weasel-worded excuse was that I wasn't ready quite yet to run the gamut of social diseases and exotic biological life sure to be encountered by probing her nether regions with my still-healthy manhood. As for the collection of tattoos located all over her well-used torso, I expressed a most philistine attitude of disinterest. "I know art when I see it," I told her, "and you are not it!"

Nonplussed, Annie would shrug off my evasions and, like the loser of the annual Tech-Georgia football game, would predict overwhelming victory next time. As for me, I considered my dodging and twisting to be signs of my adroit mind, if not of my unpredictable libido. I guess it was the time spent that mattered, and Annie usually soaked up sizable chunks of my weekends with her weird stories, all of which she swore were true.

"Shore did enjoy my trip to Floridy," she exclaimed, working on the somewhat faulty assumption that I was listening rapturously.

"'Course, it was all a mistake because of that drunken SOB Gene Talmadge Minyon. He come in here the other night, flyin' high, talkin' loud and throwin' money around like it was on fahr. Cuttin' to the chase, he said he had to go to Atlanta and axed me if I wanted to go, which naturally I did."

Throwing caution to the winds, I hazarded an interruption. "He axed you? Like what Lizzie Borden did to her step-mother and father?"

"Don't know nothin' about any Lizzie Whatever. Which truck stop did she hang out at? Maybe she blowed in from Ohier or come along before my time," she mused. "Now, shut up and let me talk. Cigarette me, bartender."

The bartender, who owned the joint and whose name was Bubba Sweat, reached into a not-so-clean shirt pocket and withdrew an S-shaped Lucky Strike. A short, stocky man with the powerful arms of a bouncer and the persona of a repo man, he ruled Bubba's with a glance and a glare. Magically, a kitchen match materialized in his hand. He scratched it briskly across his right haunch and pushed the flaring stick toward Annie's badly situated smoke. After a moment of pantomime in which neither match nor cigarette enjoyed much of a congress, the two finally merged, and Annie inhaled.

"Well, Gene told me he had to get to Atlanta pretty damn quick 'cause his rotten sister-in-law had run off with a boyfriend, and he wanted to get her back before his brother—the husband, see?—sobered up. 'I might have known that tom-cattin' Faris Trion would take to pretty little Helen,' he told me. An' he wanted me to go along to help with the driving and, well, the other usual stuff for which I am justly famous locally."

She hesitated, allowing for the appropriate arreter un instant, preened herself, and continued. "He even promised we would stop at a Motel 6 to celebrate his kicking Faris in the nuts for causing all this trouble."

"Sounds like a very civilized approach to an age-old problem," I coyly observed, dodging a cumulus cloud of nicotine-laden smoke that Annie's Lucky Strike was emitting.

"Yes, I thought it had its possibilities," Annie averred. "So, we loaded up for the trip by downing two six-packs, capped them with a few swigs of Old Grandad and piled into Gene's Studebaker Golden Hawk. It was well after midnight when we left, and with all that Dutch courage in us, I suppose it ain't too surprising that Gene was a bit discombobulated at the wheel. When we spun out onto the highway, Gene accidentally headed south instead of north!"

She paused to look at herself again in the speckled mirror hanging somewhat perilously behind the bar and over the cash register. "Gotta get some Maybelline next week," she muttered to herself, then, brightening, returned to her saga.

"Before I knew it, we was approaching Callahan, Florida. I saw the signs and tried to tell Gene, but that drunken fool kept insisting it was Cordele. Gene floorboarded that Golden Hawk, and quicker than a goose can pass gas, we was sitting in front of this ratty motel in downtown Jacksonville, Floridy."

"Well," I bravely ventured, "considering the company, that was pretty close to Atlanta. I'm surprised you two didn't end up in Bakersfield, California."

"Now, don't get me started on Bakersfield," Annie warned. "I went there once with a trucker hauling rocket fuel. Liked to throw lit firecrackers out the window while driving along to spice things up. I thought I'd end up fried like a Frito. 'Course, that trucker was a real long-distance man, if you catch my drift, so there was some compensations."

"Yes," I quickly agreed. "Your Atlanta trip to Florida certainly should have precedence. Please go on." And as reinforcement for what I knew would be a brain-twisting experience, I gulped down the remnants of my now-tepid Miller.

Pulpwood Annie exhaled a nimbo-cumulus accumulation into the water-stained Cellotex ceiling, collected her thoughts and continued.

"That place shudda been named the Roach Motel! I guess I spotted a dozen of them freeloaders checkin' out things," she said. "Gene decided he needed some horizontal refreshment and some

Old Grandad stimulation, so we ended up spendin' a fair amount of the evening putting mileage on a not-so-strong set of box springs. The only advantage was the squeaks seemed to keep them roaches at bay."

She ran her fingers through her hair and spent several moments gingerly exploring a suspicious lump or some small, living organism that had taken a fancy to her scalp. I used the pause to signal Bubba for another Miller.

Annie's bear-trap mind swung inexorably back to the story at hand, and I began to debate the possibility of securing a knockout drop from Bubba to put in her beer. She must have sensed my intentions, for she turned the can up and drained every sudsy molecule in one gigantic gulp.

"This story ought to have ended right about here," she said in a conspiratorial whisper just slightly louder than a sonic boom. "But Gene Talmadge Minyon ain't been normal since the doctor dropped him on his head at birth. He shudda gone to sleep, woke up with a hangover and then tooken us both back to Zenobia. Oh, no! He wakes up the next morning, grabs his head, gets out some little white pills and loads up!"

"Pills, shmills," I said. "What's wrong with aspirin?"

Annie drew herself up indignantly. "You stupid, overeducated jerk! Them wasn't aspirins! You ever heard of uppers?"

"You mean amphetamines?"

"I mean screaming-meemie, blow-the-top-off-your-punkin'-head uppers! Before I could even wash out my goodie, Gene was practically climbin' the walls, yellin' about what he was gonna do to Faris and Helen. And nothin' I said or did could convince him we wasn't within three hundred miles of where they were. Out the motel door we went with me pullin' my dress over my head and hoppin' along with one shoe on and the other Lord knows where!

"So, here we go, Gene poppin' an upper every few minutes and getting furiouser and furiouser as he slammed that old Golden Hawk up and down the streets. Couldn't get it in his head he wasn't cruisin' Buckhead, and he kept mutterin' that he shore didn't recall Atlanta havin' so many palm trees."

It seemed like a good time to interject some sophomoric wisdom, so I commented that maybe in the future she might try hooking up with someone who was more of a mental giant the next time she took a road trip with a trick. Like water off a duck's back, my weighty insight bounced right off Annie's brain and fell, gasping and dying, onto her cognitive floor.

"Lemme tell you something important, squirt," she said authoritatively. "It ain't no fun takin' road trips with normal people. Know why? 'Cause they ack normal!"

Well, that explained volumes and could have been full justification to shut down an insane discourse that seemed to be leading somebody straight to the Duval County Jail. Or an emergency room. Or the morgue. Being one who practiced my alma mater's decree "to inquire into the nature of things," I chose to feed Annie another question.

"What happened next?"

"I ain't so very sure. A lot went on while I had my eyes shut 'cause Gene was drivin' so crazy I didn't want to see what I was sure we would smash into. Sooner or later, Gene pulled up in front of a juke joint, said it was where Faris always hung out and without further ado went plungin' right through the swingin' doors. I followed, but the inside of that bar was so dark I couldn't see much of nothin' for several minutes. Gene started yellin', 'Faris! Faris! Come out, you no-good, wife-screwin' somethin' or other,' and in general managed to draw a fair amount of attention to himself."

As though she were providing instructions to a congenital idiot, Annie offered the following details, sotto voce cum vibrato:

"When Gene realized Faris wasn't comin' out, he and them uppers decided to fall back to Plan B, which was to start hootin' and hollerin' for the Georgia Bulldogs. 'Go, Dogs!' he shouted. 'Go, You Hairy Dogs! Go You Silver Britches!' Then, when a couple of women made the mistake of walkin' in to see what all the ruckus was about, Gene started yellin' at them, 'Go, You Hairy Bitches!' For some reason or another, their escorts took offense and informed Gene he had better start pullin' for the Gators, or they was goin' to rearrange his face by movin' it down to his rear end."

I was beginning to get the picture, and while I maintained a certain provincial sympathy for anybody fool enough to shout "Bulldogs!" in a Gator den, I also realized the perpetuator was about to receive some well-earned desserts.

"And then?"

"Well, it weren't much of a fair fight. There was two of them escorts, but there was Gene and his bottle of uppers. After all the hittin', kickin', eye gougin' and ear bitin'and rollin' on the floor was over, Gene was more or less intact while bits and pieces of the escorts could be seen all over the dance floor. Fact is, Gene was busy takin' on the jukebox when the po-lice arrived and socked him with a blackjack. Took three of them blows before Gene even felt them. He just pulled his foot from out of one of them jukebox speakers, stiffened up, yelled 'Go You Hairy Gators!" and fell face forward on the floor! Last I saw they was scrapin' him up and takin' him somewheres."

Annie stubbed out her Lucky Strike and looked around the room. She eyed a lanky yokel who had wandered into the bar and who had begun feeding quarters into the jukebox. Dollar signs appeared before her eyes, and she made motions to dismount.

"But Annie," I said. "Finish the story. What happened next?"

Annie was already moving toward the music, her antenna fixed on her next john, like a shark sizing up a plump skin diver.

"Not much else to tell," she said over her shoulder. "I drove Gene's Golden Hawk back to Zenobia, called the Duval County Jail, found out what his bail would be and sent them a money order so's Gene could get out of the slammer."

Then, she stopped in mid-floor, turned, looked me squarely in the eye, and, with an ironic smile and a wiggle of her hips, added, "After all, ain't us whores supposed to have hearts of gold?"

And so was concluded another pungent evening under the hypnotic spell of that south Georgia Scheherazade, Pulpwood Annie, whose last name I never quite caught.

Chapter 2

Regarding Pulpwood Annie's Patriotic Gesture

Archie Carter was regaling the crowd at Bubba's with his exploits—mostly sexual in nature—during his two years overseas in the Army. He was tall, blond and ruggedly built. Few would doubt he played fullback on his high school team. Fewer would doubt that he was as inept at this as was Wrong Way Corrigan. Nevertheless, rural eyes bulged as Archie waxed eloquent on such forbidden rites as "Round the World" and "Fellatio."

I strongly suspected that for most of these tractor jockeys the former suggested something vaguely involving intercourse aboard a four-engined airplane or a slow boat to China. No doubt the latter raised unspeakable concepts of copulation in a vat of Italian pasta and spaghetti sauce. So much for enlightening the masses.

"'Course, the funnest experience I had was at this brothel in Amsterdam," Archie expounded. "Went in and found only one ugly, old, fat whore just sittin' there doin' her nails. I said, 'Where's the girls?' And she answered back right fresh-like, 'Well, Buster, you are a' lookin' at them.'

"Bein' the only representative of the U.S. Army in that cathouse, I had to have a comeback. So I said, 'I was expectin' to see a whole lot of girls. Last time I was in a place like this, I had seventeen to choose from.' Figgered that would put her in her place.

"But that ol' whore was ready for me. 'Relax, soldier,' she said. 'I'll do it seventeen times with you!'"

At that, the locals broke out in roars of laughter, joining Archie in his joke. While a couple of the kibitzers pushed Archie as to his stamina if he had taken the woman up on her offer, a few more retreated to a corner to calculate just how much she'd have charged him. The consensus was she should have offered Archie a group rate.

I ordered another Miller and checked out the Saturday night crowd. Bubba's seemed to be the vortex of the usual aimless mix of farmers, logging truck drivers, mill workers, a few misplaced tourists and more than a soupcon of cracker women. These females were for the most part a rough-edged group between the ages of eighteen and forty. None came within several time zones of being the kind I would take home to Mother.

On the other hand, a couple of the more sprightly ones were not beyond my concept of, shall we say, an illicit evening of probing the intricacies of the male-female dynamic, especially since I had had a few brews. I was just getting ready to dismount my stool and head for a certain nubile redhead who no doubt was almost old enough to be where she was, when I felt a hand grab the back of my shirt collar.

"Whoa, college feller! Don't you dare take aim at that strawberry filly!"

Curses, foiled again! And by none other than Pulpwood Annie, of course.

How had she managed to sneak up on me without my having seen her? I had been in Bubba's for several hours, completely relaxed and unencumbered by the likes of south Georgia's Delilah of Defilement and Defloration. Word had it she was engaged in a business proposition with a carload of ironworkers from Scranton, Pennsylvania, on their way to sunny Florida but who were anchored for the night at the Honeysuckle Motel in beautiful downtown Zenobia. Considering what they were receiving on their three-channel motel television, I suppose they found Annie to be a more lurid, if not better, alternative. Certainly, her tattoos provided scenes never to be broadcast over the major networks.

Nevertheless, and none the worse for wear, here was Pulpwood Annie in the usually bruised and badly tattooed flesh, her face glowing with what I immediately realized was a burning desire to tell me one of her cockamamie stories. I began mentally to prepare for the worse, when I inhaled some strange and not particularly alluring aroma emanating from Annie's direction.

"Gee, what's that I smell?" I asked. "Are you still swigging Green Lizard, Annie?"

"Heck, no!" she retorted with a toss of her somewhat curly and congenitally disheveled locks. "I ain't never drunk any Mennen's After Shave Lotion in my life! Who said that I did?" She looked furiously around the barroom, scouting for the spreader of such slander.

"Well, it most certainly isn't Evening in Paris," I said. "Did some of that Yankee bay rum rub off on you up at the motel?"

"Naw," she replied, fanning herself so as to project a maximum blast of the mystery bouquet in my direction. "What you're smellin' is Atom Bum!"

"What? Do you mean you are radioactive?" Visions of cheapie Hollywood science fiction movies flashed before my eyes. Giant globules of isotope-laden tomatoes rolling inexorably toward Chicago! Herculean glow-in-the-dark grasshoppers devouring Kansas wheat fields! Pulpwood Annie the size of the Empire State Building! And about as intelligent! My mind boggled into tilt.

"No, no, no!" Annie said reassuringly. "It's Atom Bum perfume. I got it from an aluminum cookware salesman. Came by my place the other day and wanted to present a demonstration. Gave me a quart or so of this as a door opener."

She reached into her imitation lizard purse and drew forth a vial containing what looked like a septic green liquid. But it was the bottle that caught my eye. It was shaped like a miniature aerial explosive, complete with tail fins and with a removable warhead as its top. Atom Bomb was etched onto the side of the deadly looking device.

After catching my breath and coming to the realization that Annie was not a candidate to be isolated by the Atomic Energy Commission, I considered the situation and offered a sage evaluation.

"Annie, you are wearing a well-named potion. I am sure that so long as you drench yourself in this witches' brew you will never be bothered by body lice, dog-peter gnats or customers."

She was somewhat taken aback by my less-than-enthusiastic response to her scent.

"Aw-w, come on, it can't be that bad. After all, it was free, and there's plenty of it."

"So, rub it on your dog. It ought to cure the mange and screw worm infestations in a jiffy."

Annie paused and gave a reasonable facsimile of thought to what I said.

"Okay," she replied. "I'll save it for special occasions. Like when I get some of them snowbirds comin' through for Floridy. Heard no complaints from the ironworkers earlier in the evenin'."

"I hate to disillusion you, but if you had spent the last thirty years whiffing the netherworld of an ironmongery, I suspect you would embrace Atom Bomb as the essence of spring. Face it, Annie, the last time those guys smelled anything was prior to World War II! They don't have nasal passages any more, just cartilage lumps on their faces to hold up their eyeglasses."

In our numerous conversations, it was usually Annie who got in the last word. And the first word and most of the middle ones, too. Tonight's chat was definitely constituting an exception to the rule, and this meant Annie had to try a different tack. She fished out an inevitable Lucky Strike, signaled Bubba for a light, ordered a beer and told him to put it on my tab. Bubba shrugged, stared at me and walked off. Message delivered.

Annie readjusted herself on the barstool, gave a tug to her Frederick's of Hollywood black fishnet stockings, made sure nobody was within hog-calling distance, leaned close and in a conspiratorial tone began an entirely new discourse.

"I ain't told nobody else yet, but I am workin' on a special holiday offer for the Fourth of July," she said. "Ain't none of the other girls gonna have anything that'll come close!"

Although not a sampler of Annie's notorious wares, I was well aware of what she regularly marketed, usually at two dollars a pop, and quickly reached a silent conclusion. There were few females in the known world whose "anythings" would approach Annie's for lack of appeal, visual repugnance and bargain-basement price. Only a male's desperate desire for coitus explained why she was still in business. However, I did have to grant her a peculiar kind of galvanic personality, a siren-like quality that helped lure a testosterone-propelled customer to skirt toward and into her oft-visited harbor.

I bit. "So, tell me about your holiday special."

"Can't tell you. Gotta show you." Annie jumped down from the stool, took my arm in a vise-like grip and headed for the door.

It was pitch dark outside, and ebony shadows of cars and trucks crouched around the building. Annie headed for the far side of the parking lot and stopped in front of what I barely recognized as a battered International-Harvester pickup truck.

"Ain't it a beauty?" she said. "Bought and paid for it last week."

A closer examination using a Zippo lighter Annie fished from her bottomless imitation lizard purse revealed a vehicle of indeterminate age but whose bent fenders, rust-enhanced paint job, cracked windshield and missing rear window suggested it had led a hard but somewhat charmed life to be still in running condition. Frankly, I was more interested in the lighter, which had Eighth Air Force engraved on its shank. Annie snatched the lighter from me after informing me it had belonged to one of her luckless relatives who had a brief career as belly gunner in a B-17. Seems he went to sleep in the turret just before the pilot made an emergency wheels-up landing. The lighter survived more or less intact.

Gingerly, I opened the door on the driver's side of the cab and peered inside. It reflected standard south Georgia maintenance—an inch of dust on the dash and floorboard, several knobs missing from the instrument panel, a sun visor hanging at half-staff and an overwhelming odor of sweat, burnt oil, spilled gasoline and a pinetree-shaped air freshener, the latter dangling perilously from the rearview mirror.

"Nice," I said, full of genuine insincerity.

Annie ran around to the rear of the truck, dropped the tailgate and gestured theatrically. "Here's where it will be!"

I saw nothing but a dented metal bed festooned with occasional hardened cow droppings and clumps of forlorn-looking hay.

"What are you talking about? Are you planning to take your Fourth of July johns for a ride in your truck? If so, I suggest you get a garden hose and wash it out first."

"That ain't it at all," Pulpwood Annie retorted. "Lemme explain. First, the special is good only for veterans. Ain't takin' on any draft dodgers, four-Fs and Section Eights. My five-dollar holiday special will include two bottles of beer, a recorded rendition of 'The Star-Spangled Banner' by Ernest Tubb and me right here on a mattress under the stars! And that ain't all!"

Annie paused to gather up some objects hidden under a burlap sack in the back of the truck. Animated by her plan, she lay down on the bed of the pickup and began waving a slim round tube in the air.

"Try and picture this," she said excitedly. "My customer is all fired up with the beer and the national anthem. Here I am alayin' down and all spread out in the truck. He hops on board and starts doin' it for God and Country. When he gets to the really good part, I'm gonna whip out my Zippo and light this here Roman candle!"

She was so caught up in the moment that she began humping the air while igniting the Zippo and moving the flame to a fuse sticking out of the Roman candle. It caught on with a sputter.

This was something to behold—Annie bouncing around in the pickup, the truck's shock absorbers squealing in rhythmic protest, the Zippo going like the Statue of Liberty's torch and the Roman candle obviously getting ready to explode.

Now, at this point it is important to remember that Pulpwood Annie had spent most of her professional life in the horizontal position, which means she was not all that adept at dealing with the vertical. In her enthusiasm to depict her holiday special, she unintentionally let her Roman candle arm tilt not up toward the North Star but over toward the cab of the truck.

Whoosh! A brilliant red ball went arching into a nearby pine tree.

"Hooray for the United States!" Annie crowed. "Hooray for George Washington, Abraham Lincoln and Elvis Presley!"

Whoosh! A second red fireball shot forth, barely skimming the roof of the truck.

"Hooray for the Confederacy!" Annie shouted. "Hooray for Robert E. Lee, Jesse Jackson and Lester Maddox!"

(At this point, I charitably allow that Annie had badly confused Jesse with Stonewall, but there was no time for me to bring her up to speed on this delicate historical differentiation.)

Whoosh! A third incinerary went unerringly through the broken-out window of the cab, smacked into the rearview mirror, ricocheted down onto a See Rock City-labeled knob on the gear shift, caromed into the windshield and then buried itself in the seat. There, it glowered in the foam rubber padding with a menacing pink hue as tendrils of smoke began wisping up from a small but growing conflagration.

"Annie, your truck's on fire!" I shouted.

Annie's dry run terminated immediately. She tossed the still-burning Roman candle to the ground, where it proceeded to discharge seven more flaming balls into a nearby chinaberry tree, a badly situated billboard proclaiming "Good Eats at Mom's Diner," and under several vehicles in the parking lot.

"Quick!" Annie yelled. "Get some water!"

From where? All I had was an empty Miller can, and we were at the far end of the lot. A red glow began to fill the cab. Annie saw her investment literally going up in smoke.

It was a desperate situation, but Annie rose to the occasion. Down came her Frederick's of Hollywood fishnet stockings. Off came her see-through, split-at-the-crotch panties. Annie hoisted her skirt, threw open the door, hopped inside and crouched over the burning seat.

A sound suspiciously like p-s-s-s-s-s came from the cab. Smoke billowed, but the red glow turned dark and flickered out.

Coughing and gagging, Annie reappeared from an overcast of really bad-smelling smoke. She staggered over to a nearby tree and sagged against it.

"Caught that bugger just in time," she gasped.

I wish I could say the same for the chinaberry tree, Mom's billboard and three vehicles that were recipients of the holiday display. All caught fire and suffered some degree of incineration before the minions of Bubba's Bar rallied to the rescue. In the confusion, Annie and I gathered up her underwear, discreetly stayed in the shadows and kept darkness and unburned trucks between the impromptu fire brigade and us as we headed for the building.

Once safely inside the bar, I ordered two Millers and joined Annie in a booth at the far end of the dance floor. She looked exhausted but triumphant.

"Well," she ventured as she sucked on her can of brew, "I guess I need to fine-tune my holiday special, if you catch my drift."

I nodded in stunned assent.

Annie said it had been quite a night, and she was ready to head for home. I walked her out to her truck and opened the door. She got in, somewhat cautiously considering the condition of the seat, turned the key, stomped in the clutch and with an ear-piercing screech shifted into first gear. She leaned out of the window as she pulled out of the parking lot.

"The guy that sold me this truck claimed it was a real pisser," she said. "He didn't know how right he was!"

And away up U.S. 1 Pulpwood Annie clattered, trailing traces of foam rubber smoke, Atom Bomb perfume and scorched pee. My only regret was that in the hurly-burly of the evening I forgot as usual to find out her last name.

Chapter 3

Whereas the Snake and the Heifer Encumber Her Life

It was a quiet evening at Bubba's Bar until Little Paul Lowe came in with his dead snake. Little Paul was a short, wiry guy with a stubble of beard topped by dirty-looking hair he slathered regularly with Wildroot Cream Oil and hardly ever with shampoo. He sported a checkered shirt with cutoff sleeves and a pair of dungarees that looked like they had been fought over by a pack of hound dogs. Little Paul was the epitome of a typical south Georgia pulpwooder—loud, dirty, profane, at best semi-literate and perpetually horny. If a statue is ever raised in the state to honor its redneck citizenry, the sculptor could do worse than choose him as the model. But I digress.

Little Paul headed unerringly for Pulpwood Annie, his inamorata on numerous occasions and one of the reasons she had earned the appellation she bore. Annie didn't see him coming. She was focusing all her energy and her off-and-on-again allure upon two gangly high school boys who obviously were seeking to acquire something not to be confused with a Boy Scout merit badge. Somewhat unskillfully, they were negotiating a coitus session with the south Georgia Lily of Libertinism. Things had reached the point that the lads' deflowering was just about a sure thing when Little Paul sneaked up behind Annie and without a word of warning draped the snake over her bony shoulders.

"Hey, Annie! Lookie what I nailed in the swamp this afternoon!"

he shouted. "I'm gonna get a pitcher took and give it to the newspaper! 'Local Man Kills Giant Snake!' the headline will say!"

Now, Little Paul undoubtedly had more he wanted to say about his prized possession, but he didn't get the chance. Did that snake still possess a spark of life? Did something set off some postmortem muscular spasms? Did the touch and weight of the long, cold reptile trigger a kind of primitive survival reaction from Annie? Whatever. She let out a shriek that almost shattered the glass full of Miller High Life that I was raising to my parched lips. In less than a nanosecond, she pivoted, causing one end of the snake to slap into the face of her nearer potential customer while the tail swung wide and whacked Little Paul square in the mouth.

Newton's Law says, among other things, that a body in motion will continue until it encounters resistance. Well, those swinging snake ends reached their apogee and, as Annie slowed in her turn, took their cue from gravity and wrapped themselves around her neck. More yells, screams, threats of sure death and endless curses upon Little Paul's equally diminutive reproductive equipment came forth as Annie fought to disengage herself from the snake.

With a mighty heave and a whirl, she untwisted the ropy object, threw it on the floor and proceeded to stomp the remains into Bubba's battered linoleum floor with her Frederick's of Hollywood stiletto wedgies.

Another well-known law of physics says that the speed of light is the ultimate form of acceleration. However, if you had seen those two high school guys and Little Paul depart the premises, you would have truly witnessed a new method of propulsion that might well serve our astronauts as they shuttle between the planets. And I had learned something new and potentially useful. The way to get Pulpwood Annie completely distracted and also in the mood to clear out a room full of assassins was to drop a snake on her. A corollary to this, I also discovered to my dismay, was that being absent a customer or a truly stupid joker to murder, Pulpwood Annie would redirect her energies on me.

What luck. There I was, sitting on my favorite stool, enjoying

Annie's impromptu Diamondback Death Dance. Now, here she was, heading toward me with blood in her eyes.

"Make room! Move your can!" Annie shouted at the person sitting next to me. She straddled the abandoned stool, flung a fierce glance at Bubba and ordered a beer, the tab of which had my name implied all over it. She turned and continued her unprintable description of the recently departed Little Paul.

"Now, Annie," I said in my most cajoling tone, "you have to remember that it is big news in this county when somebody kills a six-foot-long rattler or grows a gourd the size of the Liberty Bell. In his Neanderthal-like way, Little Paul wanted to share his fame with you. Who knows? Maybe if you had given him a chance, he would have asked you to pose in the snake picture with him."

She mulled this over, and, slowly, Pulpwood Annie's wrath diminished as she chugged her beer. She wiped her mouth with the sleeve of her dress, but her brow remained furrowed and her mood dark. This was unusual, for it had been my experience that Annie's indifference to, naivete toward and profound ignorance of the universe enabled her to shrug off almost any weighty matter.

Maybe she had gas.

"So, what's bugging you?" I asked. "I know you are not brooding over cutting that poor snake into giblets with those awful shoes, and I know you will welcome Little Paul with open arms the next time he waves a couple of George Washingtons at you."

My class in Psychology 101 had not gone for naught. I read Pulpwood Annie like a book, pinpointed her malaise and opened the door to her recovery by means of my infallible therapeutic analysis. That is, if one could analyze Annie's often maze-like ramblings.

"Well," she admitted, "I do have somethin' on my mind. It's Great-Uncle Charlie."

Annie's Great-Uncle Charlie hung like a libidinous millstone around the neck of not only his numerous daughters and nieces but also upon most of the female neighbors who lived within hobbling distance from Charlie's farm. And hobble is the operative word here. Charlie picked up a gimpy leg by means of a rifle shot he received during the Spanish-American War. Charlie entered the annals of military history and local folklore by being the only known American who was shot while running down San Juan Hill. This is understandable if you know the unwavering cowardice that coursed like the Mississippi River through the rank and file of Charlie's ancestry. The good side of this excellent survival technique was that it put Charlie back among his many female relatives and his docile, pliable female neighbors. The result was a county full of Charlie lookalikes.

There are those, perhaps the recipients of Charlie's innumerable cuckolds, who hold the view that he would have kept his government pension and been a less frequent contributor to the area's gene pool if the Spaniard's stray round had been a bit higher and more to the middle between Charlie's fast-churning legs. But that's another matter for another day.

A second claim to fame, perhaps more dubious, arose when Charlie appeared before the county court on suspicion of incest, a charge he could have faced for weeks on end without ever encountering the same accuser twice. At any rate, after being found completely guilty of carnally knowing a daughter or some similarly close relative, Charlie faced the wrath of an outraged judge.

"How dare you use this sweet, innocent child?" the judge demanded. "After all, she's your own flesh and blood!"

Charlie scratched his butt, relocated his chaw from one cheek to the other and replied in deathless prose, "Well, judge, I never saw anythin' wrong with growin' your own pussy!"

A six-month sentence in the local jail achieved little except to provide a brief dip in the county's birth rate. Upon release, Charlie went limping back to his favorite activity, undeterred and unashamed.

So why was this aged reprobate the subject of concern from, of all people, Pulpwood Annie?

The story soon became clear, or, to be more precise, it became as clear as Annie was capable of expounding. The essence was this: Great-Uncle Charlie had been in the early throes of courting Daisy

Sapp when her husband pulled into the yard, noticed Charlie's pickup truck and speedily entered the parlor. Finding Charlie busy hiking up his pants, the husband made all sorts of accusations and dire threats. Charlie sought to defuse the situation by saying he had merely dropped by to offer for sale the fine heifer he had in the back of his pickup. Somewhat mollified, Mr. Sapp went out, studied the bovine and offered Charlie five dollars for it. Caught in a situation where he either got a royal thrashing from the belligerent Mr. Sapp or took a fin for what he knew was a fifty-dollar cow, Charlie opted for the latter. He unloaded the heifer and drove quickly away.

"Well," I observed, "sounds like a fairly reasonable business deal, considering Great-Uncle Charlie's venture into Daisy Sapp's pleasure zone. He was lucky to get the five bucks instead of a knuckle sandwich."

"Yeah, but Great-Uncle Charlie wanted to get that heifer back, felt he got cheated. And the Sapps knew that, so they put their son, Arthur Gus, in the barn to keep an eye on it. Slept in the hayloft at night with his shotgun at the ready," Annie said.

"What does all this have to do with you?" I asked.

"I'm gettin' to that."

Annie paused, bummed a Lucky Strike from a nearby imbiber, rocketed a jet of smoke into the water-stained ceiling and returned to the topic at hand.

"You see, Great-Uncle Charlie figgered it would take two to get that heifer back, and he called on one of my cousins to help out."

She mentioned the relative's name, and it rang a bell. I had seen him on several occasions, slumped over a barstool or sagging against a wall or tree. He was known more clinically than affectionately as Wormy Willie because of his debilitated state, a skin-and-bones, walking skeleton whose jaundice-like pallor and intelligence strongly resembled a bottle of Listerine.

"My God, Annie," I exclaimed, "you couldn't get five minutes' work out of Wormy Willie if you had all year! The guy has the strength and endurance of an amoeba!"

"That's what Great-Uncle Charlie discovered. Said it took

Wormy half an hour to get the truck door open, then had to take a nap to recover!"

"So?"

"So, all the rest of Great-Uncle Charlie's clan was either in jail, on escape or banged up in the hospital. So he turned to me," Annie related. "We worked up a plan that seemed like a good idea at the time."

Some plan. Great-Uncle Charlie's encyclopedic knowledge of primal lusts convinced him that if Annie sneaked into the barn and plied her skills upon Arthur Gus, the lad would be so distracted he would not notice Charlie limping in to rustle the heifer. I suppose there have been greater blunders in history rising from seemingly foolproof schemes, but few came to mind as I waited to hear how all the matter resolved itself.

Apparently, the combined seduction and heifer-napping occurred several nights back. Since neither uncle nor niece was acquainted with either astronomy or the *Farmer's Almanac,* they chose an evening when there was zero-minus light because of an absent moon and a high-altitude haze that obliterated the stars. It had also been raining.

"I waded through more cow plop and mud than I ever seen in my whole life!" Annie exclaimed with a shudder. "Finally made it up to the barn. Lights were out in the Sapp house, but when I pulled open the barn door, it creaked like Dracula's casket! And that brought Arthur Gus out right quick with his shotgun pointed straight at my belly! I had to do some quick thinkin,' if you catch my drift.

"Arthur Gus had hay stickin' all over his clothes and head 'cause he had been asleep up in the loft. Acted right surly at me and wanted to know what the hell I was doin' in his barn at that time of night. Well, I made up a story about my truck runnin' out of gas and havin' a leaky roof so I needed someplace dry to stay till the rain stopped. Saw his barn and came in."

Why was I not surprised that Arthur Gus bought that ridiculous concoction? Is it no shock to learn I was less than caught unaware when Annie said she had him up in the hayloft and thoroughly engaged in a marathon rutting performance almost instantaneously? Was I becoming such a veteran of Annie's crazy reports that I could anticipate some of their more pungent moments?

And why was I forearmed for Annie's lamentable report that Great-Uncle Charlie bungled his try at reclaiming what he considered to be his heifer?

Seems that when Charlie sneaked into the barn—no longer under the watchful eyes of Arthur Gus, who was busy pounding his maleness into Charlie's complaint niece—he made the mistake of entering the wrong stall. Instead of finding a quiet little calf, Charlie encountered a sizable boar hog. Roused from a deep sleep, the porcine quadruped snorted to his feet, sniffed the air suspiciously and spotted a shadowy figure just inside the door. Unknown to Charlie, Arthur Gus had spent his spare time poking and prodding the boar in the balls, and the animal was primed and ready for revenge. His little piggy brain sought no subtle difference between the two humans. He lowered his head, pawed the ground and charged.

Annie was unsure whether it was the door smashing, the hammy squeals of vengeful anger or the wails and yelps for help that forced Arthur Gus to disengage and to stumble toward the sounds of conflict, his manhood thrust forward like a pink pigmy spear. In the excitement, Arthur Gus forgot he was in the hayloft and proceeded to step right into the vacancy where the stairs were located, and his tumble to earth merely added to the riotous explosions coming from the boar's residence.

"I didn't know what to do!" Annie exclaimed. "I hiked my drawers, got down the stairs and found Arthur Gus rollin' in the dirt, moanin' that he had broke his dick in the fall! Couldn't do nothin' about that, but I could help Great-Uncle Charlie, so I got over real quick to where that boar had him on the ground. That ol' boar was buttin' and bitin' and stompin' poor Great-Uncle Charlie, but I managed to get ahold of his arm and pulled him up. Never saw a crippled feller run so fast in my life! Out the barn door he flew, yellin' 'Run, boys! The Spaniards is comin'!' and with that ol' boar right at his heels!"

Annie stopped in order to replenish her memory with a swig of her beer.

"Well, the boar chased Great-Uncle Charlie 'round that barn two or three times before they headed for the road where Great-Uncle Charlie had hidden his truck," she said. "Luckily, he had left the tailgate down on the pickup, and when Great-Uncle Charlie jumped up onto the bed, that ol' boar scrambled right up behind him!"

Annie scratched behind one of her ears and took another drag on her cigarette.

"You know, you jes' gotta give my uncle credit for thinkin' on his feet," she said sagely. "Soon as he saw that boar in the truck, he hopped down, slammed the tailgate shut, cranked that sucker up and drove off! Left me standin' in the rain, havin' to listen to Arthur Gus hollerin' about his injury. 'Bout that time the Sapps got wise to the commotion, and lights began comin' on in their house, so I took that as a cue and hauled buddy up the road!"

As usual, this Pulpwood Annie tale left me flabbergasted. What else could have happened? Since when did one of her stories screech to a halt with only these incidents having taken place? Surely there was more. At any rate, I had to ask.

"And after all that?"

"Well," she replied archly, "all I got out of it was a few right unsatisfyin' humps from Arthur Gus, my hair full of straw and a head cold from walkin' back home in the rain."

"And your uncle? What did he do with the boar?"

"At first he toyed with holding that ol' boar for ransom, but he figgered the Sapps would just call the sheriff and get the animal back. So he decided to hide the evidence. Knocked that boar in the head, had him quartered and scalded quick as a wink and was busy gnawin' on a king-sized batch of pork chops before you could say lickety-split!"

"Yes," I observed, "but when I first saw you, you were expressing concern for your uncle. Sounds like he came out of the fray pretty much ahead of the game. Except for the whipping that boar gave him."

"I suppose you could say that," Annie countered. "But Great-Uncle Charlie came out too much ahead 'cause he ate so much of that pig that he got the worstest case of indigestion and the squirts ever a man had in this county! Ended up swallerin' I don't know how much paragark, Pepto-Bismol and even had to have his stomach pumped out! He's been feeling so porely it's even cut into his love life!"

Annie got down from the stool and took steps toward what passed for the ladies' room at Bubba's, but before reaching the door, she turned and provided me with a final insight into the celebrated incident.

"Guess what? For all my help, my Great-Uncle Charlie didn't give me any of that boar 'cept his balls! Said they was prairie oysters! Just wait and see if I ever help him steal a heifer again!"

And with that Annie disappeared into the toilet. It was time I left, stunned at the revelation, and it was only when I was miles from fabulous Zenobia that I realized I again had failed to find out Annie's last name.

Chapter 4

Pulpwood Annie and the Three Wise Men of Zenobia

Humbug, Grunt and Rooster Paulk were to miscalculation and mistake what Curly, Larry and Moe were to anarchy and mayhem, and the twin curses followed them like dark, sinister clouds as they traversed tiny Zenobia, Georgia, in search of work and pleasure. Their problems had started early. The ejecta of several generations of shiftless turpentine workers who had drifted in from Robeson County, North Carolina, to brutalize coastal Georgia's virgin pine forests as they had already done throughout the Tar Heel State, the three cousins first saw light in adjacent tarpaper tenant quarters in one of the less swampy areas of Zenobia's largest land owner.

They grew up accustomed to newspaper wallpaper to help keep out the cold, a steady diet of salt pork, collards and iron-tainted well water and a Sears Roebuck catalog to conclude the daily regimen in a nearby outhouse. Humbug was the oldest, Grunt was a year younger, and Rooster arrived a year after that. All had shiny black hair, dark eyes and a pallor that strongly suggested their recovery from hookworm and/or pellagra had not been entirely successful. Running around barefoot winter and summer no doubt contributed to their endemic, parasitic condition. Their diet took care of the rest. They also possessed more than a touch of Lumbee Indian blood, a byproduct of their ancestors' having merged occasionally with Robeson County's Native Americans, people whom white North

Carolinians saw as being considerably below them and scarcely above the recently freed slaves.

No matter. Amidst the shacks of the Tillman Quarters, the Paulk boys were viewed as being as equally scabrous and unpromising as were the other white children who played in the dust and mud. That is, if anybody gave a thought about Humbug, Grunt and Rooster at all. Their fathers had disappeared down Brunswick way after having said they were going to work in the shipyard during World War II. Perhaps they boarded one of the Liberty ships and got torpedoed by a lurking Nazi submarine. Their mothers also took advantage of wartime circumstances, relocating to Jacksonville to claim various factory jobs and to whore on the side. None of the parents returned. The boys stayed behind with a common grandmother.

Being the eldest, Humbug quickly became the trio's self-appointed leader. It was he who became inspired after viewing a Saturday afternoon cowboy movie. The western actor, Charles Starrett, who wore a black outfit and mask and was known as the Durango Kid, specialized in hopping off buildings onto his trusty white stallion, then galloping away after crooks and cattle rustlers. The stunt looked easy to duplicate.

The boys borrowed a neighbor's obliging plow mule and arranged it strategically below the second-story hayloft opening of the neighbor's barn. Grunt held the mule by the bridle while Rooster provided the countdown near the mule's tail. From the hayloft, Humbug then hurled himself into space, spraddle legged, and landed with full force and no padding onto the mule's razor-sharp back. Startled, the mule brayed mightily and kicked both rear hooves outward, catching Rooster in the chest. Three backward flips later he ended up in a pile of fresh manure.

However, Rooster certainly suffered less than did Humbug, who had his cajones severely banged and battered upon impact with the rock-like, muley target. Indescribable pain spread with the speed of light throughout Humbug's scrawny body. Struck silent in agony, he slowly slumped to the left and dropped with a most un-Durango-Kid-like thud onto the ground, where he cupped his bashed gonads tenderly and hoped for a merciful death.

Meanwhile, Grunt struggled unsuccessfully to control the terrified mule and ended up being slung into a barbed wire fence, from which he received certain interesting and stinging wounds.

It will come as no surprise to those who have grown up with pineknot-hard country kids that the Paulk boys survived and prevailed. Humbug developed a rather slow, elliptical style of walking for the next two months, Rooster took a bath long before his regular Saturday night plunge, and Grunt found he drew all sorts of attention and admiration by having his wounds covered with oversized Band-Aids.

A lesson unlearned is apt to be a lesson repeated.

In due course, both Rooster and Grunt found to their dismay that their form of play and adventure could also lead to undesired results. During one of those rare periods when the Paulks actually attended the Zenobia public school, they discovered to their amazement and delight that the building possessed plumbing. This novelty provided endless opportunities to turn on water spigots, flush toilets and throw rolls of toilet paper into whatever receptacle happened to be available. Even more fun loomed when they discovered that the boys' room toilets backed up to a wall that also had the girls' toilets on the other side. Soon, a small hole at the top of the wall was mysteriously expanded, and boys took turns shinnying up a water pipe to observe what was occurring on the other side.

Alas, when Grunt climbed up for a look, the rusty old pipe snapped loose. Grunt plunged backward and landed in a galvanized steel bucket the janitor used when he mopped the floor. Combine the height of the pipe where it broke and Grunt's weight at the time, and you can imagine the velocity with which Grunt's rear end impacted with the bucket. Would you be surprised to learn the bucket caved in partially, and that hapless Grunt found himself wedged firmly into what remained of it? Yelps of fright and pain brought needed help, but the help just stood around and shrieked in laughter at Grunt's painful predicament. For months afterwards, Grunt possessed a large, purple circle around the circumference of his gluteus maximus. The offending zero also symbolized his new-found disinterest in academe, and his school-day attendance record soon shriveled to nothingness.

Not to be outdone, Rooster earned his place in the annals of Paulk family screw-ups when he attempted to drive his grandmother's old 1937 Plymouth out of the dilapidated garage in which it had been parked. Unfortunately, Rooster knew as much about shifting gears as he did about performing ballet. He put the Plymouth into what he thought was reverse, turned his head to see where he was backing and proceeded to drive forward and through the garage as well as the attached tool shed. Two punctured tires, a smashed windshield and horribly mangled hammers, rakes and shovels were the beneficiaries of this venture, and Rooster shook glass shards from his hair for weeks.

Then, there was the time the boys found a discarded pogo stick. The protective rubber stopper was missing from the steel rod that connected with the spring to give bounce to the pogo stick. No matter. Grunt hopped aboard and commanded Rooster to pull down on him to get a better bounce. The system worked well until Grunt gyrated off the concrete and onto the ground and in the process pinioned Rooster's right foot with the steel rod, piercing the fleshy area between the big toe and its neighbor. The rod was firmly wedged both into the soil and between the toes, giving Rooster a sort of maypole to run around like a demented Morris dancer, yelling his head off in pain.

After studying their cousin's predicament for a while, Grunt and Humbug pulled the pogo stick from the ground, thereby freeing Rooster, who ran to Granny Paulk for aid. She poured Absorbine Jr. on the open wound, creating a new series of shrieks and hop-abouts, but by that afternoon Rooster was ready to play shortstop in a pick-up baseball game conducted in a nearby vacant lot.

Having eventually grown too old for mandatory school attendance and too large to remain living in Granny Paulk's tiny shack, the three decided to strike out on their own. They quickly found that there was little work for three uneducated adolescents with no discernable skills or the capacity to learn such skills if the opportunity prevailed. The Army recruiter hooted when the trio showed up at his door and volunteered to help defend the country. And the county school board showed unexpected sagacity when it turned down the Paulks' offer to work as janitors at the Zenobia schoolhouse.

Luckily, when all else seems to fail in south Georgia, there is a safety net, and it is working on a pulpwood truck. This nasty, dangerous, low-paying, insect-plagued, snake-infested, muscle-wrenching job attracted the region's rogues, parolees, wife-beaters, petty thieves and others of similar ilk and persuasion. It was thus to this last-chance opportunity that Humbug, Grunt and Rooster turned, and it was through this work that they became acquainted with the redoubtable Pulpwood Annie—the reigning queen of south Georgia prostitutes.

At first, the Paulks had to dedicate every earned penny to pay the rent on the hovel they now occupied and to acquire such essentials as cooking utensils, mattresses, food and beer. Nature, however, demands that more than one appetite be satiated, and it was not long before the testosterone-laden Paulk boys began to desire that which a willing woman is best suited to supply. Hardly any of Zenobia's young females had such low standards as to include the Paulks in their social connections, and it was through this inevitable process of elimination the Paulks soon concluded their only hope for respite lay in Annie.

I was aware of and sought whenever possible to avoid any of Annie's feckless clientele. They were inevitably smelly, loud, profane and strong enough to whip my fanny seven ways from Sunday. Only my insatiable thirst for alcohol prompted me to run the gauntlet of unshaven chins, red-rimmed eyes, bruised knuckles and ragged checkered shirts when I entered Bubba's for a liquid repast.

I first became aware of Annie's involvement with the Paulks when, on an evening that was otherwise glorious, she stomped into Bubba's, fuming.

"Well," I greeted Zenobia's Debutante of Debauchery, "I see you are waxing ill under a veritable thundercloud of uncheer. Prithee, what could be the cause of thy distemper?"

Annie ignored my masterful use of Elizabethan jargon. Instead, she yelled for a Miller, eyed me furiously to communicate I was to pay for it, swallowed half a can in one prodigious gulp, burped and straddled the nearby stool.

Having firmly established her ire and her place in the Bubban firmament, Annie chose to reply.

"It's them damn Paulks. I just hate doin' bizness with them!"

"Now, now," I purred smoothly. "Since when has Zenobia's walking Red Light District taken to a quality control check on her customers?"

"Phooey!" she exclaimed. "Just goes to show what you know! I got standards, just like ever'body else!"

And with that, she hiked the strap of her skimpy Frederick's of Hollywood mini-dress—a purple number decorated with large yellow bull's-eyes into which very male-looking red arrows were inserted—and continued.

"I have tole them and tole them. You want to do it with me one at a time, at least one of you has gotta have bathed first! I don't know why, but Humbug, Grunt and Rooster have such a dislike for soap and water!"

Inspiration murmured in my ear.

"Annie, I have a solution. What you need to do is get in touch with the nearest Holy Roller preacher. Have him on hand next time the Paulks show up horny. Tell them they have got to be baptized before you take them on. Once they get dipped, they ought to be at least one coat less dirty and smelly than they were before that preacher dunked them in the creek."

Annie gave me a look that strongly suggested I had had my mental oil checked and had been found several quarts low.

"No, thanks. I'll figger something out."

And that's where we left the issue for the evening. However, on my subsequent visits to dear Zenobia and to Annie, I kept being brought up to date on the latest imbroglios into which the Paulks were inexorably entwined. Annie was fast becoming the Louella

Parsons of the Humbug-Grunt-Rooster circle.

The initial news was that Grunt had had his hand squashed while helping load a log onto a truck. Disabled, he began scouting around for another job and lucked into doing deejay announcing at the local radio station after the star of the airwaves, Elmer Creamer, had retreated to Savannah for a long-overdue hemorrhoid operation.

Unfortunately, Grunt's encounter with the printed words was limited pretty muchly to Tijuana Bibles and menus at drive-in cafes. Even with one hand in a sling he could cue up records and punch in cassettes, but when it came to reading things like commercials and the local news, he quickly hit shoal water. Announcing standards at one-thousand-watt AM stations in the South are not all that rigid, but one is supposed to be able to master certain basic things. Grunt's first gaffe occurred while plugging a long-playing record of favorite songs. He glibly proclaimed that the disc contained "the nineteen top tits of the nation!" Then, upon realizing his slip-of-the-tongue, he snickered and chuckled on-air through the rest of the program while the telephone switchboard lit up like a Christmas tree from either eager purchasers or horrified gentry.

Annie was particularly proud of his announcing that in a local 4-H contest a certain young female was "the top hoer." Edging weeds from the bean patch was decidedly not what the maiden was described as being, and Annie said with a snort of laughter that she did not consider the girl to be competition anytime soon. However, Grunt's fifteen minutes of fame came and went after he plowed into a local newscast and described a certain well-known female pillar of local society as the virgin wife of the mayor. Being as Grunt's knowledge of geography was virtually nil, he did not understand the subtle difference between the state of Virginia and the synonym for chaste and untouched. Not surprisingly, his pink slip was immediately forthcoming.

Meanwhile, Humbug was experiencing a cash flow problem. Seems his paycheck flowed from his pockets shortly after getting into a poker game with some of his pulpwood associates. Needing money for just about everything, including a quickie with Annie, Humbug sought what he termed "an unsecured loan" by breaking into the local Western Union office and rifling the drawers for loose change and blank money orders. Fingerprints all over the office and imprints of his size-thirteen clodhoppers in the dirt outside the window Humbug broke open gave the sheriff all the clues he needed to throw Humbug into the local jail.

This ante-bellum structure was suited more for corralling goats than it was for restraining felons. As soon as his cousins passed a crowbar through the bars of his window one night, Humbug managed to pry the cell door open enough that he could slip out. Fortunately, he was the only prisoner, and no law officer slept in that small, odorous lockup. Humbug's plan was to break into the Western Union office again, steal a few things and leave a taunting note for the sheriff. This, he figured, would "prove" that someone else, and not he, had done the original break-in. Unfortunately, when Humbug tried to re-enter his cell, the crowbar popped loose. The still-locked door snapped to, pinning Humbug and his pocket full of Western Union property to the doorframe. And this is where the sheriff found him the following morning, half suffocated and with a permanent crease across his chest and back.

"Guess ol' Humbug will be cleanin' out ditches in the county for the next few months," Annie confided. "Just to cheer him up, I sent him a rain check for his next go-round with me. Can't say them Paulk boys is much between the sheets, but of the three, Humbug's the least worst!"

My intellectual horizons having been expanded in trigonometric proportions by this latest bit of licentious reporting, I grabbed my can of Miller and drained it to the dregs.

With Grunt unemployed and Humbug an unwilling guest of the county, this left Pulpwood Annie to deal with the remaining Paulk. Not surprisingly, Rooster made several noisy forays into Bubba's during the succeeding months, chatting up Annie and indulging in her specialties whenever he had managed to acquire two dollars and was reasonably close to his most recent bath. Annie kept me informed of all the details, most of which were so crammed with prurient and debauched activities that I could scarcely take notes.

Time flies, and after an absence from Zenobia while the Georgia Bulldogs exerted themselves through another less-than-perfect football season, I returned glumly to Bubba's with reminders of the latest Tech victory resonating painfully in my brain. Of course, I encountered Annie astride a barstool, a bent Lucky Strike dangling from her lower lip.

"I am downwind, and I do not detect a discernible aroma of Paulk maledom and dirtdom," I coyly observed. "Has your allure been going south, dear Annie?"

She deftly exhaled a fog of atomized nicotine that spiraled into the ether of Bubba's sub-stratospheric ceiling, yawned and slowly cut her ruby-tinged eyes my way.

"Haw! I ain't doin' bizness with them guys no more," she said.

"My, my, how picky you have become of late. Did they try to pay you for a trick with a Confederate dollar bill?"

"Not on your life. They upped and left town."

I commented that their departure made sense. Annie had kept me informed of Humbug's jail commitment and of Grunt's memorable radio mispronunciations, and I observed that perhaps the Paulks would find their fortune somewhere over the horizon.

"At least, Rooster left with his skirts clean, so to speak," I added.

"I wouldn't say so," Annie commented, almost as an afterthought.

"Oh? You mean the youngest of those rounders also got his tail in a crack? Do tell me more."

Well, according to Annie, Rooster started picking up extra pocket change on weekends by mowing the yards of Zenobia's rich and famous. As luck would have it, he was doing the mayor's lawn when His Honor's recently maligned wife looked out the window, observed Rooster's shirtless, sweaty torso and gave way to an irresistible coital impulse. When the mayor came home early for lunch, he discovered the Mrs. and Rooster in what can only be described delicately as a compromising position.

Shouts, screams and the sound of punches thrown echoed along the tree-lined street. When things quieted down, the mayor was sporting a fat lip and a black eye, his wife was packing her bags and seeking a bus ticket to carry her back to ol' Virginny, and Rooster was making plans to depart Zenobia posthaste.

"Luckily, Humbug was out on parole, so he and Grunt convinced Rooster to go with them down to Floridy," Annie said. "Last I heard they was signed up with some carnival and was livin' in that little town near Tampa where all the carny people go during the winter."

I had relatives in Tampa, and I knew of what she spoke. Gibsonton, a tacky little fishing village on the Bay just south of Tampa, was the off-season mecca for every carnie roughneck and freak who had ever had a lengthy connection with the country's notorious side shows, thrill rides, three-card-monte games and hoochie-coochie exhibitions. One of its earliest mayors was an eight-foot-tall skeleton billed as the World's Skinniest Man. Naturally, his wife was the Bearded Lady.

Gibtown! What an enlightened choice for those misfits! There, they could meld into the population without creating a single raised eyebrow. With neighbors like the Lobster Boy, the Two-Headed Baby, the Fat Lady, the Alligator-skinned Boy, the Human Blockhead, the Monkey-faced Girl, assorted midgets and dwarfs, tattoo artists, tin can tourists, sword swallowers and glass eaters, Humbug, Grunt and Rooster would have finally come into their own.

"Nature has a way of balancing things out in the end, don't you think?" I observed. "The Paulks have found their calling, and, at least, you are free of those gamey guys and won't have to wear a clothespin on your nose while doing a trick."

"Not necessarily," Annie replied. "I got a postcard from them the other day. Said they would be back in Zenobia this fall when their carnival arrives for the county fair. They wanted to renew our bizness arrangement. Guess I oughtta honor their advance reservations."

Well, that was Pulpwood Annie for you. I suppose one should consider her and her calling something like that famous line associated with the Statue of Liberty, for unto her came the tired, the weary, the smelly and those seeking a release from that for which Annie was only too glad to arrange. For two dollars, that is.

I thanked Annie for her update on the Paulks and dismounted the stool I had occupied during her discourse.

"I probably won't be back in town until basketball season is over," I said. "I understand the Bulldogs have a killer team and are aching to whip Tech's butt. I want to be on hand for that, for sure."

"Well, so long, college boy," Annie replied. "Give them Dawgs my best. 'Course, if they ever come down to Zenobia, I'll be glad to do it personally."

I struggled to imagine the university basketball team's reaction to Zenobia and, even worse, to the likes of Pulpwood Annie. By the time I had decided such an encounter was as unlikely as my making the dean's list, I discovered Annie was disappearing out the door with an unshaven guy with red-rimmed eyes, bruised knuckles and a torn plaid shirt.

And, alas, I had again failed to extract from Annie her last name.

Chapter 5

Concomitant to Her Partnership in the Travel Industry Bizness

Pennick Ravi Patel, a short, skinny man with dark skin, darker eyes and an even darker outlook on life, sought manfully for the great American Dream. Having persuaded friends, relatives and other mutual contacts to invest their money in him, he immigrated to this country and immediately zeroed in on the Honeysuckle Motel, which a wily south Georgia realtor had been pushing unsuccessfully for months. Located on U.S. 1 just south of Zenobia, Georgia, it had been a gold mine for the original owners, Elwood and Mildred Labronski, who gladly abandoned the arctic blasts of Willard, Wisconsin, in order to open a then-new concept of tourist lodging in the sunny South.

The years between 1927 and the 1950s had been good for the Labronskis, but they learned early about President Eisenhower's interstate highway scheme, studied a road map and realized quickly it would avoid U.S. 1 like the plague. They decided to sell out, for even at that date snowbirds were abandoning the old tourist roads for the segments of divided highway rising up like ribbony dragons' teeth along the Georgia coast.

Now, who would be fool enough to buy a non-franchised and somewhat dog-eared motel on a dying tourist highway but an East Indian completely ignorant of what the future foretold for his purchase? And so it was that Pennick Ravi Patel sank all his borrowed cash into the Honeysuckle Motel while the Labronskis took the money and ran with great dispatch to a senior citizens' enclave in Opa Loka, Florida.

The good news for Pennick Ravi Patel was that the first month's gross at the Honeysuckle Motel was pretty impressive. The bad news was that subsequent months rarely measured up to the first, and in painful geometric progression the returns provided less and less with each thirty-day period. It was not long before Pennick Ravi Patel was having trouble making monthly payments to his relatives, friends and other contacts back on the dusty plains of Mother India. Asiatic courtesy prevailed at first, but as fewer and fewer dollars arrived to be converted into rupees, those who had invested in the Honeysuckle Motel began to express great concern.

One night, Pennick Ravi Patel received a telephone call in which a voice hissed menacingly that full payment had better begin immediately "or ve vill sleet youa throt!" Visions of curvy, steel-bladed knives waving in the multiple hands of Shiva disturbed Pennick Ravi Patel's sleep for many nights thereafter. Seeking to avoid a fatal encounter with some dagger-plunging Punjabi thug, Pennick Ravi Patel began considering a kind of partnership to increase his cash flow as well as his chances for seeing dawn rise regularly over the pine trees, if not over the Ganges.

Pennick Ravi Patel decided that since one of his most frequent guests was Pulpwood Annie—that exotic dispenser to the dissolute, debauched and desperate—she might be the answer to his financial problems. It was his proposal to her on this topic that led to my being involved.

Now, the Hindus may have invented the concept of karma, but it was I who lived it regularly. When I came over to Zenobia for refreshment, I usually ended up being engulfed in one or more of Pulpwood Annie's wild and absurd situations, all of which involved her in some kind of destructive or demonic venture and all of which she claimed were gospel truth. Yes, it was my karma to endure ratchet-jawed Annie. Fate, you are a real sonavabitch at times. But I digress.

Having abandoned the University of Georgia in order to spend a weekend in my alcohol-challenged home town, I soon developed a strong thirst and bummed the family car for a quick trip down to nearby Zenobia. I had scarcely pulled into the parking lot when Annie came flying out the door of Bubba's Bar and began rattling away excitedly about what I barely understood to be something about a motel and some "bizness" deal she had going. I did my best to brush her off in order that I could escape into Bubba's and slake my parched throat with a soothing brew. I was so used to Annie's blather about the nuts and bolts of her unsavory life that I paid little heed to this latest eruption.

In my most gentlemanly manner I told her to stuff her problems where the sun rarely shined, to get out of my way and to talk to me only after Bubba Sweat and I had experienced an exchange of cash for a can of Miller High Life. "Then, maybe just then," I said, "I may be able to tolerate your rantings." Annie clung to my heels, sulking but obviously also tingling with some item of earthshaking importance.

Have I said that I was a favorite of the slatternly Annie although I determinedly chose to avail myself of zero percent of her questionable and oft-used charms? Instead, and despite myself, I developed a malignant fascination for her conversation.

Scrunched onto a barstool and whispering into my shell-like ear with the intensity of a hurricane and a volume akin to Mahalia Jackson at full gospel cry, Annie brought me up to speed.

During one of her stopovers at the Honeysuckle Motel and following a quick post-coital wash-up, she was wandering across the parking lot when Pennick Ravi Patel beckoned for her to come into the motel office. Thinking she was in for another quick cash bonanza, she went in only to learn that the motel owner wanted to talk about his business, not hers. Or at least, not directly.

In a high-pitched, clipped voice, he explained he needed more customers and pointedly encouraged her to bring her trade there as often as possible. Annie said that was a good idea being as she was tired of getting her bones bounced on the flatbed of pickup trucks, in the cab of lumber rigs and behind every bush and bramble in south Georgia. Pennick Ravi Patel then pushed for his more desired objective—someone to provide venture capital to help sustain the motel "until ze torist trade peeks op." Did Annie know someone who might be interested? He assured her it was a potential gold mine, and he would share some of the predicted bounty with her, if....

Turns out Annie did. One of her most regular customers was A. Pickett Poindexter, a lightbulb-shaped individual whose financial empire embraced a Pure Oil Station, a funeral parlor and a cemetery situated on the region's most worthless, sterile land. Each had a history untarnished with worthy intent. A mistaken tire order in the fall of 1941 had left Pickett with an inventory of 120 dozen tires instead of the twelve he had ordered from Firestone. This proved a bounty after Pearl Harbor, and he waxed rich selling bootleg tires on the black market until the Georgia Bureau of Investigation got wind of the scheme. Eight months behind bars in Reidsville did little to mitigate Pickett's avaricious intent, and when his dear old grandmother died at the age of ninety-one, he quickly acquired a mail order embalming license and turned her wooden frame house into a funeral parlor, Granny being the first customer. And her estate being tapped for the expenses.

A lucky hand in poker had provided him with five acres of such arid unpromise that they would be considered rejects for the Great Sonoran Desert. Pickett cleverly decided that just because back-to-back cotton crops since the Civil War had sucked the soil of everything but sand and clay, there was no reason he could not make a profit by planting products from his funeral parlor in "gardens" six feet long, three feet wide and six feet deep. Plus, he could sell markers, most of which turned out to be hideous pink marble monuments shaped like engorged hearts and on which were inscribed lachrymose verses universally unsuited for the unlettered deceased reposing below.

In short and in sum, Pickett was bringing in the money and needed outlets for investment just as he needed outlets for his male urgings. His wife, Deanna Mae, was barely four and a half feet tall and constituted the most apparent concentration of ugliness to be found in female form within a six-county span. Not surprisingly, he turned easily and often to Pulpwood Annie because of her access, low maintenance and, for what he considered in his limited sexual repertoire, her rapacious appetite for him. Considering his best comparison was the repugnant Deanna Mae, Pickett may have been right.

"So," said Annie, "I told him about the motel partnership offer, and ol' Pickett burnt rubber drivin' out to talk about it. 'Course, he was right familiar with the Honeysuckle bein' as that's where we usually go to do it. He and that Indian struck a deal, and Pickett put up five thousand dollars for a twenty percent partnership with the option to get another ten percent until he is half owner! Ain't that great?"

I had not just fallen from a turnip truck. I knew that Interstate 95 was already siphoning out-of-staters from the old thoroughfares like U.S. 1, U.S. 17 and U.S. 301, and I did not have to be a mathematics major to deduce that falling revenues produce red, not black, ink.

"Annie, I hate to be the one to burst your bubble, but you are hitching your hopes to a dying horse, and so are your so-called business partners, Gunga Din and Bartlett Pear," I soothingly replied. "Plan your retirement income elsewhere."

Annie demurred in a somewhat pithy rejoinder, not only saying I was wrong but also indicating what part of my anatomy she wanted to excise for my having suggested such a blasphemy. I hastened to say she was unfocused and biased on the subject, and I had no plan to undergo any alteration of my most treasured spot just because my prediction proved true.

There the matter rested, just like an argument between Georgia and Georgia Tech fans over next year's post-Thanksgiving football game. Months passed, and then one evening when I was in Zenobia quaffing a few for the good of my liver and kidneys, I saw Annie burst into Bubba's. Naturally, she headed my way, elbowed the girl sitting next to me at the bar, straddled the just-empty barstool, bummed a cigarette, ordered a beer for my tab and began rattling away.

"I'm flush!" she exclaimed, reaching into her imitation lizard purse and pulling out a Michigan bankroll of what seemed to be one- and five-dollar bills.

"I'm so impressed," I replied. "With that wad, you can dine on R.C. Cola and Moon Pie for ages. Pray, how did you come upon this bounty?"

"It's my bizness partnership at the motel, stupid!" she rejoined, and without waiting for my gasp of astonishment, she continued.

"I've been double-dipppin'! I been takin' all my customers to the Honeysuckle, where they pay me and for the room, of course, and afterwards the Indian gives me a cut of the rent. But listen! I been gettin' the other girls to take their bizness there, too, and I get a piece of that action as well!"

Almost out of breath, Annie stopped to drag on her cig and chug a bit of her brew.

"Us workin' girls has been pullin' in the customers! Been keepin' that ratty ol' motel full most every night, if you catch my drift!" she boasted.

I was amazed. And then I got suspicious.

"Hey," I said, "where is Mahatma Ghandi getting all that cash? If he needed a partner, and most especially if he had to reel you into the deal as well, then he was definitely experiencing a cash flow problem."

Annie spent a nanosecond in pondering my question.

"Don't know, but the best news is that ol' Pickett Poindexter has got so excited about the new bizness that he's upped his payments to the Indian and is about to buy him out, lock, stock and barrel."

What Annie didn't know, and what I learned only much later was that Pennick Ravi Patel was cooking the books—using Pickett's payment for part ownership to bribe every whore in south Georgia to bring their customers to the Honeysuckle. He shared only the "check-in" statistics with Pickett and "reluctantly" allowed the greedy undertaker to buy more and more of the motel until, at last, the entire facility was Pickett's.

Freed at last from this albatross, Pennick Ravi Patel bought a one-way ticket back to Bombay, where he was perceived as a rich American who could afford a house with running water and a servant or two. He promptly married the first of a series of Punjabi women, all of whom died in mysterious "kitchen fires" after having produced an endless succession of female babies.

As an unwritten part of the motel sale, Pennick Ravi Patel also made contact with a certain Madjul Vishra Patel—no relation—who purchased a round-trip ticket from New Delhi to Savannah, Georgia. He rented a car there, paid a visit to the Peach State Gun and Knife Emporium, where he purchased a curvy steel blade manufactured in Bangladesh, and then drove to Zenobia. He checked into the Honeysuckle Motel and returned to Savannah the next day for his flight back to India.

It was Pulpwood Annie who broke the news to me shortly afterward. The minute I sashayed into Bubba's, she was at me, beside herself with excitement.

"You missed it! You missed it! Serves you right for spendin' all that time up at the university 'sted of stayin' at home and payin' attention to what's goin' on down here!" she shouted.

"What on earth are you babbling about?" I asked while trying manfully but futilely to belly up to the bar. Had she become a Jehovah's Witness and launched a career in dispensing *The Watchtower* to irate suburban housewives? Had a quantity of south Georgia's whores moved to south Florida, thereby measurably raising the intellectual level in both states? Had some Yankee dipstick proposed marriage?

"The knifin', that's what!" Annie said with a snort.

Lacking any female intuitive powers, I remained firmly in the dark. Knifings along the strip south of Zenobia were hardly news, especially on Saturday nights.

"Okay," I said, "fill me in. The last knifing I heard about involved Caesar at the Forum."

Annie ignored my thrust at literary parallels. Instead, she began filling me in on the incident. Seems an unknown person broke into the residence of A. Pickett and Deanna Mae Poindexter and assaulted the latter with a long, curvy knife. The assailant's apparent intent was to slash Deanna Mae's throat, but being short and in the dark and resembling a somewhat chunky fireplug, she presented a confusing target. The man swung his blade from left to right at what he discerned was her neck. Instead, he managed to render a swooping, superficial slash from ear to ear and directly in line with Deanna Mae's mouth. Unnerved by his victim's vigorous and extremely loud reaction, especially after having whacked what he considered to be her windpipe and carotid artery, the attacker beat a hasty retreat.

"I think I even got a look at him," Annie confided in a hoarse whisper. "I was just finishin' up with a customer at the Honeysuckle when this car comes wheelin' in real fast. Out jumps a strange lookin' guy...resembled Daddy Warbuck's bodyguard, you know, in the funny papers."

That clue was sufficient: tall, dark, mean-looking, wearing a turban.

"Can't nobody figger why he cut Deanna Mae," Annie added. "She was homely enough before gettin' her face sliced."

I could "figger." That rat, Pickett, had made as part of the motel purchase deal an agreement that Pennick Ravi Patel would send back somebody to relieve Pickett of his pig-faced wife. Only the guy missed and made a truly bad situation worse.

Or did he?

I had reason to ponder that as I started to leave Bubba's later that evening. Annie was in her cups and was eyeing a tourist from New Jersey who was loudly bragging about his billiard-playing ability. Little did he know his "Joisy" ass was about to be taken in more ways than one. Before moving in on Leo Gorcey, she offered the opinion that Deanna Mae's injury may have been a blessing in disguise.

"First of all, ol' Pickett got so upset seein' all that blood and hearin' all that screechin' that he started feelin' sorry for the way he had been treatin' Deanna Mae. After gettin' her face stitched up, he started takin' her to the motel and lettin' her run the registration desk," she said. "Once the cuts healed, Deanna Mae and her scar tissue constituted the biggest smile in south Georgia. Them tourists must like it 'cause more and more of 'em stop off every night. Sometimes I can't even get a room for my regular bizness!"

The resolution of this horrible mess stunned me, and I walked out of Bubba's trying unsuccessfully to sort out the kind of cosmic logic that would have set in motion the events leading up to the finale Annie had described. Imagine! Surgical Southern hospitality!!

I gave up. Some things are not to be understood by man. Only by a whore like Pulpwood Annie, who was always remiss in providing her last name.

Chapter 6

Pulpwood Annie and the Minnesota Ice Maiden's Legacy

A sun-baked summer in south Georgia is seldom fun. However, when you factor into it a month of sweaty labor in a hot, smelly tobacco warehouse, ticketing bales of bright-leaf tobacco for the company that bought it for cigarettes, cigars, chewing tobacco plugs and snuff, well, you get the idea. I was not garbed in white linen and continually engaged in sipping mint juleps at afternoon soirees. The silver lining to all this, quite literally, was that the work put coins in my pocket. Coins that could be converted into beer in nearby Zenobia.

Not that Zenobia was always at the forefront of my thoughts. On evenings after work and during weekends I betook myself as often as possible to the estate of my cousin, Lulu. She had flaming red hair, a turned-up Irish nose, delicious-looking freckled cheeks and a set of jugs that would have aroused envy from Jayne Mansfield. Three years younger than I, Lulu also possessed a lively personality, a host of nubile female friends, a swimming pool and a tennis court. How could I resist?

Unfortunately, I wore my welcome out one afternoon in late July when, during a violent game of doubles, I fired my usually uncontrolled return volley across the net at near-jet speed. Instead of whiffing the back line of the tennis court as it was intended, the furry round missile soared straight for Lulu's melon-like left breast. The resounding smack, followed immediately by wails, yelps and an uncomplimentary choice of curses pouring forth from the injured Lulu, indicated my presence amongst her social set was decidedly truncated.

When one door closes, another often opens. In this case the affable swinging aperture was at Bubba Sweat's bar in crusty, dusty Zenobia, where an enlightened county commission allowed the legal sale of alcoholic beverages. Surrounding counties, totally intimidated by the arctic temperance winds emanating from their Baptist and Methodist churches, stood as one in favor of Prohibition. Naturally, all the Baptists, Methodists and assorted heathen types sneaked over to Zenobia when money and thirst coincided. It was a broad and well-beaten path that I followed, once the luxuries of Lulu's domain became off limits.

Having frequented these fleshpots often during weekends when I was home from the University of Georgia, I pretty well knew what to expect. I paid homage to the American Legion, home of the famous twenty-five-cent Canadian Club and Seven-Up highball, eyed the usual suspects congregated at Kelly's and then aimed the family sedan at the lumpy dirt parking lot that graced Bubba's like a grayish-brown bib. Maybe I could sneak in, drain a can of Miller's and escape before that cheerful chippie, the ineffable Pulpwood Annie, laid her bloodshot green eyes on me.

Since I was for some unfathomable reason her favorite, I usually had to suffer her brassy company whenever we both showed up in the same place. On this occasion, however, she was absent. I thanked the gods of chance and had a fine evening. Several other visits provided similar soothing results. Eventually, I became somewhat disturbed by Annie's absences. Like an undesirable habit, she radiated a kind of mystical allure to which I ultimately succumbed, although I always limited things to conversation. Every offer, every appeal that I tumble into her two-dollar-a-pop arms received my firm, and usually indignant, rejection. Still, Annie's continued absence from Bubba's and Zenobia's other tosspot emporiums finally prompted me to make a few discreet inquiries.

"Hey, Bubba, where the hell is Annie?" I shouted over the roar of a jukebox full of Ferlin Husky records, a television blasting an announcer's breathless account of some wrestling match and the babble of several dozen loutish customers.

"She's got a boyfriend!" Bubba replied in a voice that probably carried down to the Florida line. "Ain't seen her in weeks." Bubba then turned and uncapped a longneck for a Lon Chaney Jr. clone, who was pounding his hamlike fists on the bar.

What?! A boyfriend?! I had long supported the theory that there was no woman so ugly, so fat or so old that she couldn't find somebody to stick it into her, but the concept of a regular sweetie for the likes of Pulpwood Annie boggled my mind.

It was amazing. Talking to Annie usually caused my brain to boggle. Now things had deteriorated to the point that news about Annie had the same effect. I trembled at the thought of my vulnerability.

Well, every dark cloud has its silver lining, and if Annie were to be in absentia because of some obviously blind, deaf and halt boyfriend, who was I to complain? The rank and file of the pulpwood truck driver corps could find some other babe to ball. I would enjoy the calm and peace of a beer without having to look over my shoulder in dread of a certain south Georgia prostitute entering the building and my space. And conning endless beers at my expense.

Another appropriate cliché is that every good thing must come to an end. One evening, I sauntered into Bubba's, claimed my favorite seat at the bar, ordered a Miller and settled in for the evening when, WHAM! a hand slapped sharply upon my sunburned back, and a welcoming whoop shattered the calm. Pulpwood Annie was back with a vengeance.

"How good to see you again, Annie," I somehow managed to respond, my voice reflecting more than a tincture of authentic insouciance. "What foul circumstance brought you back to this neck of the woods?"

"Wasn't no chicken truck, thank you very much!" Annie retorted. "I drove over in my pickup, like I usually do!"

I declined to translate the difference between "foul" and "fowl," deciding instead to apply upon her certain superior metaphysical skills I had secured from Psychology 101.

"So, where have you been all this time? I can't believe the money I've saved from not having to pay for your drinks," I murmured.

"Don't wanna talk about it," she said doggedly, which meant, in Advanced Annie, that she was dying to spill everything.

I signaled Bubba, and a can of Miller magically appeared. Annie grabbed it, drained a fair amount in one gargantuan gulp, slammed the can down and began to unload.

"I've been spendin' time with Denny Eichelberger," Annie said. She smiled and attempted to strike a boastful posture, but her nerve somehow failed, her chin trembled, and two enormous tears discharged themselves from her eyes. Gathering speed, the tears cut wide furrows in Annie's overly done Maybelline makeup. They paused at her jawline, then dropped onto the top of her flimsy Frederick's of Hollywood Daisy Mae-style, polka-dotted peasant blouse. There, they glimmered briefly before soaking into the cloth like two flattened acorn caps.

"I jes' can't help it!" Annie said with all the emotion of Joan Crawford having to choose between a slimy Zachary Scott lounge lizard and a noble George Brent hero. "We was jus' right for each other!"

She snuffled a bit, cleared her nostrils with the aid of a paper napkin, readjusted her underwear and continued her discourse.

T'was not a pretty picture. It seems one Dennis Eichelberger of the pre-Revolutionary War Deerfield, Massachusetts, Eichelbergers had been summoned to a town near Zenobia, where he explained to a wealthy land baron the intricacies and advantages of a certain newfangled product. Denny was a sales representative for Kontiak Incorporated, one of the now-forgotten manufacturers of first generation computers. The Kontiak XIII gained brief fame as being the company's first computer to run long enough for Underwriters Laboratory to give it a conditional approval. Which explains what happened to Kontiaks I-XII.

The land baron wisely avoided purchasing the expensive, unwieldy and probably unreliable/inaccurate Kontiak XIII, and Denny glumly prepared to return to his home in Chagrin Falls, Ohio, and his wife, Selene. Which on the surface was strange, because Selene Gustafson Eichelberger was one of the most beautiful women in the Buckeye State. A tall, shapely blonde with piercing blue eyes, a heart-shaped face and a complexion made for the covers of *Cosmopolitan* or *Vogue*, she was a walking sexual icon that, unfortunately for Denny, was all bark and no bite.

They met while attending Slippery Rock College. He was a Massachusetts Brahmin, and she was a second generation Norwegian from Mankato, Minnesota. He thought she was Brigette Bardot, Mamie Van Doren and Sandra Dee rolled into one. She thought he was as harmless as her fairy hairdresser. Both missed their fantasies by a country mile.

This Denny found out on his honeymoon night, when Selene strongly resisted as he tried extending his hand beneath her thick, wool nightie. The outraged bride stiffly informed her new husband that theirs was supposed to be a "spiritual" relationship, not to be sullied by that awful physical stuff. Denny persisted and eventually succeeded that night in triumphing over the "spiritual," but Selene never forgave him, and she never forgot.

Future romantic efforts at the Eichelberger residence were met with four lines of defense. Selene used "daintiness" to delay or sidetrack the snorting, aroused Denny. "It's so, well, so sticky!" she would say. "I don't like to feel sticky down there."

When that failed, she fell back upon "distress," bemoaning the loss of "spirituality" in their marriage. Denny understood "spirituality" like he did brain surgery and would continue to lunge, cajole and generally seek to pin poor Selene to the nearest bed, chaise longue or breakfast room table.

The third line of defense was "disdain." In moments of Denny's high sexual frenzy, Selene could project "cold" that would have impressed the Birdseye Frozen Food Company. "What a tiny little weenie you have," she would say to the flushed and ready Denny.

"Why don't you visit the doctor and see if he can give you a salve you can rub on it to make it bigger?"

All else failing and a connection foregone, Selene would close her eyes and think of some icy Scandinavian fiord. After Denny was spent, she would jump up, dash into the bathroom and douche herself *mit Aryan wirkunsgrad, energisch und der fleiss*. Needless to say, there were no little Eichelbergers running around the house to despoil Selene's quest for "spirituality."

It was this sense of sexual frustration, coupled with a company rep's sagging morale when a sale goes south, that Denny brought with him to Zenobia. Taking a room at the Honeysuckle Motel, and in the process being momentarily stunned by the ragged but Olympic-sized smile that the ugly little female desk clerk gave him, Denny freshened up and drove to Mom's Diner. There he faced an indigestible round of greasy chicken, rock-hard biscuits and a collard greens-and-okra combination that even Julia Child would hesitate to prepare. Dyspeptic and disillusioned, Denny then drifted down U.S. 1 and by chance stopped in at Bubba's Bar for a nightcap. You can guess whom he encountered.

"I was out lookin' for a customer, any kind of customer, when Denny walked in," Annie continued. "God! He was so good-lookin'! Curly hair! Dimple in his chin! I thought maybe he was a movie star, 'cause he reminded me of Gene Autry or Fernando Lamas, I forget which."

It was obvious that Annie's eye for faces could lead to comparisons and conclusions for which my psyche was not prepared that evening, and so I sought to divert her back into the mainstream of what I was sure was another delicious, decadent adventure.

"Yeah, yeah, Gene or Fernando, I'm sure. So, what happened next? Did he get out a bottle of Flit and squirt you with it?"

"No, silly," Annie replied without flinching a whit. "He just walked over and asked me if I wanted a drink."

According to Annie's version of the evening, the pair instantly clicked. Beer followed beer, quarter followed quarter into the maw of Bubba's noisy jukebox, dance followed dance and cohabitation followed that. SOP for the fabled Pulpwood Annie. What was not standard was the continuation.

Denny Eichelberger was living, walking proof that no good deed goes unpunished. When he first met Selene at Slippery Rock, he was so enamored that he gladly accepted her endless delays and "saved" himself for what he was sure to be his Night of Nights in the not-so-distant future. Thus, his experience in the fleshly arts was pretty muchly limited to what he finagled and/or manhandled out of the reluctant Selene. Getting a sexual partner like Pulpwood Annie was, for him, like playing a slot machine that hit "jackpot" with every pull of the lever.

"We did it ever which way you can imagine," Annie recalled with a smile of pleasant recollection. "Frontwards, backwards, sideways, upside down, inside out, you name it, we did it. Over and over again. Day after day. He said he'd never had it so good!

"Matter of fack," she added with a boastful grin, "I stopped charging him by the trick or the hour. Gave him my weekly rates!"

From what I was able to extract from Annie's libidinous account, Denny kept delaying his departure for Chagrin Falls. Therefore, she stayed with him in his inelegant Honeysuckle Motel room, leaving only for rounds of gourmet-deficient dinners at Mom's Diner, bouts of drinking at Zenobia's various dives and, occasionally, driving around the area in Annie's beat-up old truck.

"Only reason we went a'ridin' was to give Deanna Mae Poindexter a chance to change them sheets at the motel," Annie inserted as an aside. "Denny said them sheets was gettin' too many peter tracks on 'em!"

All would have continued indefinitely except for the fact that Denny's boss became worried because his crack salesman had not reported back from deepest, darkest south Georgia—an area he considered as a combination of Lower Slobovia and the killing fields of Harlem and the Bronx. He phoned Selene to find out where Denny was and discovered she did not know, either. Concerned that her prime source of income was AWOL, Selene began making telephone calls and eventually traced Denny to the Honeysuckle

Motel.

Unfortunately, when she called Denny's room, good ol' Pulpwood Annie answered, thinking it was Deanna Mae with some morsel of gossip. Stranger conversations have seldom occurred on Ma Bell's lines:

"Hello?"

"Well, a great big hello yourself! What the hell is a'goin' on up there at the front desk?"

"What?! Who is this?"

"Who do you think it is, Eleanor Roosevelt? It's Annie! How cum you callin' me while I'm busy with my boyfriend?"

"What?! I beg your pardon. I obviously have the wrong room!"

CLICK!

The telephone rings again. This time Annie gets in the first word.

"Hey, Deanna Mae! You gonna get somebody in trouble! You just connected somebody's wife to me and Denny's room!"

"What?!"

"Hey, you sound like that woman I jus' got through talkin' to. Hey, lady, better tell Deanna Mae at the front desk to connect you with the right room! Bye!"

"What?!"

CLICK!

Sounds of a telephone ringing furiously.

Perhaps, it was some stray strand in Denny's medulla oblongata that sent forth a primitive survival signal. Whatever. It was he who wrestled the telephone from Annie's sweaty paw, and it was he who spoke into the receiver.

"Yes?"

"What?! Denny?!"

"What?! Selene?!"

The rest can be imagined. Shrieks of accusation! Sputters of clumsy cover-up! When the diatribe cum alibi concluded, Denny was left sagging against the headboard. He dropped the telephone receiver limply onto the freshly stained sheets.

"It was my wife. She's coming down here to bring me home."

After that, there was no joy in Mudville, for mighty Casey had struck out. At least, according to Annie, his bat had deflated, which, I suppose, leads to the same conclusion.

"So, what happened next?" I asked, knowing a Pulpwood Annie story never ends at a logical point.

Annie finished her beer, got up and stretched, giving her Frederick's of Hollywood outfit a good testing of its tensile strength. Fortunately for the crowd at Bubba's, everything held together and kept her fetid female charms from either showing or flopping out.

"Not much else to tell," Annie rejoined. "That woman got down here in a New York minute and chewed poor ol' Denny up one side and then the other. Then, she took him to the Waycross airport for a flight up to Atlanta and points north."

"Good riddance to bad rubbish," I cleverly observed. "Consider yourself blessed that Denny's wife didn't take a razor to you. After all, that's common payback in this neck of the woods."

"Phooey! That woman wouldn't know how to use a razor 'cept to shave her legs!"

"But surely she had something to say to you! After all, you had been sexing it up with her husband for weeks! I would think she would have bawled you out, if nothing else."

Annie gave me a look that inferred a kind of universal smarts possessed only by certain gifted females, such as herself. And no males, especially a smart-alecky college kid like me.

"Matter of fack, she did have a few words with me, but not what you might think! Said on the flight down she did a lot of thinkin' about the situation. Decided maybe it would be better to divert Denny rather than just try to avoid him."

Annie paused, lit a Lucky Strike and blasted a damp morass of smoke in my direction. I ducked and immediately added two-point-five days to my lifespan. She continued.

"Yeah, Denny's wife figgered that since her husband had finally gotten a real taste of what he had been pesterin' her for, he would not be satisfied with her no more. But she didn't want to lose her meal ticket. So, she axed me if I knew any workin' girl up in Chagrin Falls,

Ohier, that I could recommend for Denny to use when he's horny. Told her I shore didn't but would get the word to her first chance."

She got down from her stool and prepared to leave, but before departing she added a final comment.

"Gotta get over to them truck stops outside Ludowici. Lots of women work them stops, and maybe one would like to catch a ride up to Ohier and start doin' trade in Chagrin Falls. After all, I kinda feel I owe it to Denny's wife to get him properly connected!"

With that, Pulpwood Annie flounced out of Bubba's and into the night. I heard the growl of her beat-up International-Harvester pickup truck, the clash of gears and the squeal of her tires as she hit the blacktop.

"What a woman!" I thought. "Wonder why I never can remember to ask what her last name is?"

Chapter 7

How Pulpwood Annie Helped Derail the SBM & A Line

The miscellany of life affords a wondrous opportunity for the unexpected. This certainly was true each time I bumped into Pulpwood Annie, that non-pulchritudinous perpetuator of pineywoods passion. Her gamey customers, her incestuous relatives and her trashy friends seemed to constitute numbers that would rival the plankton in the sea. And each was a story more lurid and lusty than the last.

Such was the case of *pere et fils* Hovis and Jervis Crummey. Both frequented Annie regularly, and it was not by coincidence that they appeared together in Bubba's, seeking you-know-who for you-know-what. This is because the two men worked on the same train for the same railroad.

Nepotism was the least of its worries for the infamous Savannah, Brunswick, Macon & Atlanta Line, a notorious travesty of a railroad that wandered aimlessly around and across much of southern Georgia before making a half-hearted stab northward toward that armpit of the Peach State—Macon—and then up to its capital. Those who had tried to do business with the SBM & A Line claimed its letters stood for Slow, Bumbling, Mismanaged and Antiquated, and they were the ones who were being kind.

It was whispered that a shipment of the Confederate gold was once lost somewhere along its wobbly, less-than-parallel-track route.

However, even the hoboes who occasionally chose a wrong ride and found themselves proceeding at a glacier-like pace across the pine barrens didn't bother to follow up on this misplaced bonanza rumored to be lurking somewhere amidst the SBM& A's rickety, clattering cars.

Just how Hovis Crummey qualified as a train engineer is beyond the understanding of normal men. Tall and bony and sporting tobacco-stained teeth within a thin, weathered face that resembled the actor John Carradine on a bad day, Hovis was an early candidate for the delirium tremens school of substance abuse. He drank corn likker before going to work, during work, after work, during his occasional bath, while engaged in sex and even at church. Only the SBM & A's fear of union seniority rules kept the owners from having sacked him years ago.

Somehow, Hovis persuaded the line to take on Jervis after he had completed his sophomore year football season at Zenobia High. Maybe the leadership sensed that Jervis would help keep his father on track—metaphorically and literally—in case of trouble. As might be expected from the limited and unimaginative south Georgia gene pool from which he was cast, Jervis turned out to be short, fat and nearsighted. And so, this Mutt and Jeff team became an enduring part of the SBM & A.

The goings-on involving Hovis and Jervis Crummey would never have entered my sheltered life had not Annie come forth with the gory details one evening while I was unsuccessfully engaged in buying the minimal number of Millers, during which time she hit me for one after the other. It was a slow night for Annie, professionally speaking, and she took up the slack with lucky me and my straitened wallet.

"Yessiree Bob, I usually got 'em comin' and goin' on a night like this," Annie observed while inhaling her third can of the Champagne of Bottled Beer. "Can't figger why nobody ain't callin' on me for some service."

"Perhaps the public health department has issued an all-points bulletin on you," I sympathetically responded. "I suspect you are right up there with that in-crowd of diphtheria, Brill's Fever and pellagra.

Maybe your photo is down at the post office with the other most wanteds."

"Phooey on you!" she said. "This is your big chance to do it with me while there ain't a line waitin'. And here you sit, nursin' that glass like it's the only one you can afford."

Annie's clairvoyance never failed to amaze me, although I did conduct a surreptitious check in my pocket to see if any overlooked change remained to fund another brew. As usual, nada.

Ah, but there was a silver lining to my dilemma.

"Not that I would, of course, but I am flat broke now that you have sponged that last drink off me," I quickly said. "Since when have you begun providing freebies to your followers?"

The very idea obviously incensed Annie's cockamamie set of values.

"I ain't never give it away!" she informed me in Darth Vader-like overtones. "And don't you go hintin' I should do otherwise! No smart-aleck college boy is gonna get away with that!"

The indignant Annie then proceeded to dismount from her less-than-steady barstool and to straighten out her dress. It was the usual conglomeration of tacky splendor that Frederick's of Hollywood had made a fortune selling to women whose "charms" usually negated whatever tantalization the garment may have possessed. This one was a yellow ensemble that plunged south and charged north with little remaining in between. What there was of it was decorated with phallic mauve earthworms emerging from red mons venus-like eruptions. Added to this distracting display were fluttering, sequined toucans and great crested grebes that seemed to be pecking away at the protruding Genus Lumbricii. God knows what the Freudian symbolism meant. Fortunately, my course in Ornithology 101 enabled me to identify immediately those misplaced birds and their inappropriate dinners.

I refrained from a critique of her abominable garb. Instead, I foolishly sought to re-ignite the conversation.

"Here, here," I said soothingly. "The thought never entered my mind."

Annie was as easily consoled as she was offended. She crawled back onto her stool, negotiated another mighty sip from her glass, flashed me one of her better all-is-forgiven smiles and resumed her discourse.

"Well, if you can't do it, you might as well hear about those what can. Whadda you want to hear about first?"

"Please! No more stories about your Juke and Kallikak relatives!"

"Got no relatives by that name and wouldn't tell the likes of you if I did!"

Mercy, like uranium salts, comes in microscopic amounts. I breathed a small sigh of relief.

"*Muchas gracias,*" I said. "I feared I was about to be railroaded into another Great-Uncle Charlie fiasco."

Railroaded! That's all it took.

"You want to know about railroads? I'll tell you about railroads," Annie quickly rejoined.

Where the lore of prostitution and railroading merge is around the ruby-lensed, kerosene-fueled lamps that early railroad men carried as they walked the yards at night and checked the cars. Many of these lanterns were often docked temporarily but burning fiercely outside the whorehouses found in most towns of any size at all, while their owners sampled the corporeal wares therein. Soon, those places came to be called red light districts.

Although red lanterns were obsolete and retired by the time Hovis and Jervis came to work for the railroad, they continued the earthy tradition their predecessors had set by regularly utilizing easy women in the villages, towns and cities along the line. Annie was one of their more reliable and accessible ones, of course.

Certainly, that's the way Annie told it to me.

"Ever time I heard that ol' SBM & A engine come chuggin' into town, I knew one of the other of them would likely show up around here, wantin' me while he waited for the train to be loaded or refueled. Regular as rain, they was!" she recalled.

I gathered that the local sock factory, which employed several of Annie's more coordinated and less-likely-to-be jailed relatives, provided the bulk of the SBM & A's cargo in these parts. A screaming need from K-Mart for cheap anklets would mean a nice stopover in Zenobia for the Crummeys. And a few extra dollars for Annie.

Considering that the southern part of Georgia was crisscrossed with a number of railroads, including the Southern, the Georgia and Florida, the Central of Georgia and the Seaboard Air Line, it can safely be assumed that any train bringing its workers anywhere near Zenobia gave its crew a chance to get to know Pulpwood Annie. Legions of railroad men seemed to fill her mental little black book, and I sat spellbound as she recalled names, times, places and intimate positions involved with each.

"Lord! Them railroad men shore are a horny bunch!" she exclaimed. "I think they must 'uv got on the telegraph and radioed their friends to come by and see me. Never had it so good than when them railroad men come into town!"

"That being the case, I am surprised you aren't flaunting an oil can and grease rag to use on your customers. While wearing a striped engineer's cap!" I chimed in.

Annie pondered that one a little too long for comfort but finally shook her gnarly hair in sad rejection.

"Naw, I better not do that," she said. "Might piss off some of my customers in other professions."

I envisioned farm hands, truck drivers, Spanish-speaking green card holders and sleazy tourist types forming a brotherly boycott in front of Bubba's. Somehow, I felt she was safe from any irate picketers, unless they were wives and sweethearts whose husbands and boyfriends were regularly diverted Annie's way.

As with many of Annie's beyond-infinity stories, she tended to drift into the fringes of what I found to be most interesting—namely, her splendidly sordid intercourse with her male "clients."

"Hey, get focused, Annie!" I demanded. "Tell me more!"

This is where Hovis and Jervis entered the picture.

Annie rolled her squinty, red-rimmed eyes around the room, plucked a moist-looking Lucky Strike from her less-than-generous bosom, pulled out her battered Eighth Air Force Zippo, somehow set fire to the cig and took a long, unhealthy drag on it. She was obviously scraping barnacles from her recollection of unprintable railroad-related raunchiness. I could hardly wait.

Annie quickly covered the usual encounters with the men at the dives along U.S. 1. And the "bizness" she had with each. No big news there. However, the story got more interesting when she delved into the marathon drunkenness that Hovis often manifested when rutting.

"How could he perform when he was slosh-full of rotgut booze?" I asked.

"Don't rightly know, but it was a right common thing for ol' Hovis to show up with a pint in each back pocket and another tucked into the bib of his overalls. And that don't account for what he had poured into himself before arrivin' here," she said. "After we was through, he would stagger off, bottles empty, back to the rail yard to drive his train up the road."

I observed that this was information more useful to the Women's Temperance Union than to a randy guy like me.

"Well, you shoulda been here the day he came roarin' in here, celebratin' the latest raise the union had got for its workers. Called on drinks for the house, took me in a taxi to the Honeysuckle Motel and then proceeded to work on a fifth of Canadian Club. Never saw a man drink so much in my life!"

She paused to reflect happily upon the moment.

"After a while, even ol' Hovis began to feel the effects. Tongue got thick, said the room was spinnin', rolled around on the floor and never did figger a way to get back up on his feet. I finally gave up and left him a-wallerin' there and went out to the front desk to talk with Deanna Mae. Figgered I'd get my bizness done with Hovis when he sobered up a tad."

"I am underwhelmed so far with this story, Annie. Surely your lifestyle has not retreated into what I would consider a typical day in south Georgia. Blue-collar riffraff flopping about in an alcoholic daze is not what I consider to be on the cutting edge of local history!"

At this, Annie became indignant.

"That's jes' like you smart-aleck college boys! Always in a hurry and missin' the big picture! Hold your horses 'til I get done!"

Okay, I was properly chastised. I slurped on my Miller and sulkily aimed an ear in her direction.

Annie cleared her throat, struck what she considered to be a dramatic pose, readjusted a strap on her minuscule dress and continued.

"If Hovis had had a different job, things wouldn't 'uv got out of hand. Seems like it was several hours after we got to the motel that Jervis come runnin' up, lookin' for his pa."

At this point Annie got so into the story that the events tumbled out, ass over elbow, and took a surreal, contorted spin. I had to straighten out the narrative later. What it amounted to was this: Hovis's absence from his train was about to set an SBM & A record for tardiness. A big order for socks had been on-loaded, and it had to be in Atlanta at a certain time to be transshipped to all the K-Mart stores in that part of the southeast. And here was the train engineer smashed out of his gourd, unable to sit up, much less stand, and covered with fetid emissions oozing steadily from every orifice.

There was no option for the son. He would have to cover for his father. Jervis took one last look at the miserable hulk that was Hovis, who was now into the dry-heaves stage of his recovery, and sped out the door.

Now, Jervis Crummey was still serving his apprenticeship as axle-greaser and general rail yard flunky. During his regime of caring for the train, he had either nearsightedly overlooked oiling the wheels on one of the boxcars, or—more likely—the ancient set had finally rusted into oneness. With Hovis at the helm, this would have been discovered and resolved safely as soon as the locked wheels began to throw sparks. Hovis would have disconnected the car and left it at the nearest town—SOP for the railroad, even one as badly operated as the SBM & A.

When Jervis mounted the engine and shoved the lever into "forward," he had only two thoughts on his mind: to get the socks to Atlanta and to prevent any SBM & A people from knowing that

Hovis was AWOL.

The train was scarcely a mile north of Zenobia when friction from the frozen wheels generated the first spark. After that, the conflagration grew as the train reached top speed. If the drag from that car's impacted wheels caused the train to go fractionally slower, it was not noticed by the frantic, myopic, self-appointed engineer.

If, if, if.

I have often wondered which of those badly located "ifs" might have prevented the events that followed. A biggie was if there had not been a record drought in Georgia that summer. It had not rained for weeks, and everything was tinder dry. Naturally, the drought was accompanied with a daily breeze that stirred the torpid air while giving little relief to the heat.

It was the breeze acting in conjunction with the sparks that started what became the longest forest fire in the Peach State. Soon, every stand of pineywoods, every dusty pasture and every blackberry patch along the SBM & A line was smoldering, then flaring into flames.

"Lordy! From what I heard, it was like Sherman was marchin' backwards through Georgia with a firebrand in each hand!" Annie said. "There was fires all the way up the state!"

Another big "if" was if the SBM & L line had run near towns instead of snaking through endless woodlands and farm areas, somebody might have noticed the fire-emitting train and the blazes springing up in its path. Not so. What few houses were near the line were all too often without telephones, or the inhabitants were disinclined to get involved, or they were plowing some distant field and didn't notice the smoke until it was too late.

What few towns that were served by the SBM & A began getting confused telegraph and telephone reports about the fires, but these all arrived long after Jervis had steamed by in a blaze of glory, like Phaeton arching the sky in his father's flaming sun chariot. Finally, calmer and more logical heads pretty well figured out that the train was causing all those fires to the south, and calls went out to the SBM & A's Macon office to do something about it.

The line's primitive communications equipment was located in the caboose that brought up the rear of the train. This was where Jervis normally rode, but since he was at the helm, there was nobody to get the message when Macon frantically signaled for the train to stop damn quick. As a result, Jervis brought his sparkling load into and through Macon in a memorable pyrotechnic display that almost ignited the Wesleyan College campus.

Meanwhile, in Atlanta, the line's top brass was huddled in a desperate effort to forestall the train somehow and to figure out exactly what to tell the media types who were beginning to place annoying calls to the main office about certain mysterious conflagrations. There were no connecting rail extensions between the SBM & A and its rivals, making it impossible to shuttle the train onto a siding where it could burn itself out in isolation.

With the usual wisdom involved in a committee decision, the group determined that the only way to stop the train was to park some automobiles across the track.

"Get the police or the state patrol to put one of their vehicles astraddle the nearest crossing, turn on all the lights and sirens and flag that sonovabitch engineer down!" the president instructed.

They tried it at Barnesville. Unfortunately, the crossing occurred directly after a sharp curve in the tracks. Jervis rounded the corner going full blast and whacked the police car into the bushes without even knowing what he hit.

Farther up the road in Forsythe, Jervis mistook the sheriff's souped-up black Ford for a shadow from nearby trees. After a noisy impact, the train dragged the car and the surprised sheriff some two hundred yards before the battered vehicle hit a bridge abutment and spun off the tracks. The sheriff announced afterward he would not stand again for re-election.

As for the effort to roadblock the train several miles north in Stockbridge, a psychic state patrolman sensed the train was not about to stop and pulled his patrol car off the tracks seconds before Jervis blew through. Sparks from the angry wheels singed the trooper's "Smokey the Bear" hat.

Certain facts began to click into place in my cranium. I recalled hearing several years ago about a train setting fire to woodlands across the state. I had no idea it started in Zenobia and certainly was not prepared to learn that Annie was somehow involved in the disaster. On the other hand, I shouldn't have been at all surprised.

"So," I demanded, "how did it end? Did Jervis start the second Burning of Atlanta?"

"Nah, nothin' like that," Annie replied. "Seems them locked wheels got so hot they melted and fell off just shy of the Atlanta train terminal. Jervis had the engine runnin' at top speed, but it wouldn't move because the car collapsed on the rails and blocked the train from movin' any further. Started a fire in some of them wooden boxcars and smoked up that load of socks something fierce. Understand K-Mart put 'em on sale at half price!"

"But what about Hovis? Didn't he get fired for dereliction of duty?"

"Naw, naw. Remember, he was a union man. The union argued Hovis wasn't at fault 'cause he was drunk at the motel with me. They docked him a day's pay! He was back to work the next day!"

"Then how about Jervis? Surely he was held responsible for the most spectacular fire since Rome burned under Nero!"

"College boy, you just ain't got no imagination. Of course, they couldn't do nothin' against ol' Jervis. He wasn't no engineer, so the union argued he couldn't be held responsible for doin' a bad job at engineerin' the train that day. If you ain't nothin', how can you be responsible for doin' what you ain't?"

Annie's rhetorical question inflamed my mind with its blatantly illogical conclusion, but who was I to question union policy?

"Okay, okay. I won't pursue that line of thought any further. Is that the end of the story?"

"'Course not," Annie responded indignantly. "After Hovis sobered up a little bit, me and Deanna Mae tossed him in the shower and washed him down good. Gave him a few rounds of my specialty, collected my fee and went on to other things!"

"And that was the end of things?"

"Not quite. All them fires generated a rash of lawsuits. The SBM & A couldn't handle the costs and went bust. Sold out, lock, stock and barrel. Some Japanese outfit bought the rails, the engines and all them metal wheels, shipped the whole mess back to Japan and melted them to make them little Toyotas and Datsuns you see all over the highway nowadays. Guess the SBM & A is back in Georgia, after all!"

The evening was providing its usual overload for my delicate senses. Drunken and near-blind train engineers! Great balls of fire across Georgia! Reconstituted railroad equipment in the form of Japanese compact cars! Pulpwood Annie at the root of it all!

While Annie worked on rearranging some fragment of her flimsy dress, I chose the moment to slide off my stool and slink unseen out the door, through Bubba's parking lot and into the family car which—thank God!—was not Japanese in origin. I was so relieved to be free of Annie and her latest story that I didn't bother to fret that I had failed again to seek out her last name.

Chapter 8

When She Participated in th' Weddin'

Midterms were mercifully over! Darling buds were poking out of the winter-battered limbs of a few Athens trees, and it was time for spring break. The lucky and the rich headed their beer-laden cars toward Daytona and Fort Lauderdale. The unlucky and impoverished went home. Guess where I ended up?

Oh, well. There were some microscopic compensations. For me it was Zenobia, the crusty little burg that boasted more beer joints per capita than any of the other small town entities that had penetrated and survived in the south Georgia pine barrens. And not that far from my alcohol-deficient home town.

As soon as I had paid homage to my suspicious relatives and had gotten my laundry washed, I mowed a few lawns, pocketed the pay, scrounged the family car and headed down U.S. 23 for my favorite oasis. Well, not really. The Zenobia American Legion, which prided itself in never turning away a veteran or any white person who at some point might possibly have been in uniform, was closed for repairs—a euphemism for massive renovations following a world-class, Saturday-night-wipeout fight. There would be no more twenty-five-cent Canadian Club and Seven-Ups for me this trip.

I reluctantly motored down the road. A herd of Harleys parked in front of the Green Grotto convinced me my chances of completing spring quarter in one piece diminished in geometric proportion for each minute I spent in that hellhole. Bye, bye, Green Grotto.

Things at Kelly's seemed equally unpromising as I surveyed the pickup trucks and badly dented pre-World War II sedans nestled up to the building's glaring, blinking neon trim. Something told me that gritty bunch would welcome a reasonably clean collegian about as much as they would fire ant bites on their peckers. Not my kind of crowd, thank you very much.

So, that left Bubba's Bar, and this meant I would more than likely run into that jolly jade—Pulpwood Annie. This strange-looking and somewhat addled woman gave prostitution a bad name to just about anywhere except south Georgia. As luck would have it, Annie had a fixation on me. In fact, she would often walk away from a surefire two-dollar trick in order to regale me with some bizarre report on her life or that of her shady sisters in the trade. Listening to her usually gave me a headache. Or made my eyeballs feel as though their anchoring tissues were gradually ripping free. Still, she had a malignant allure that I had to admit I could seldom resist. Not for her misused and undoubtedly exotically infected anatomy but for her convoluted, inexplicable and wholly unbelievable stories. Which she always swore were true.

I took the plunge, pulled into Bubba's roller-coaster-like dirt parking lot, situated the car near a beat-up logging truck and ambled into the building. I quickly occupied a stool at the end of Bubba's genuine imitation pineywood bar, ordered a Miller and cast a wary eye over the crowd. My bonny blues locked on two red-rimmed, squinty grey-green orbs connected to the grinning face of Pulpwood Annie, who was riding herd over Bubba's hillbilly-music-laden jukebox. She stuffed a coin into the slot, punched in a Hank Williams and headed missile-straight for me.

"Yore Cheatin' Heart" came blasting from the speakers, and Annie mouthed a stanza and did a few boogie steps before giving me her usual warm greeting.

"Well, college boy, it's about time you showed up. I've been saving a two-for-one opportunity jes' for you!"

"Good Lord, Annie," I suavely replied. "I'm so overwhelmed that I will offer you twice your usual fee to forget you ever hit me with such a completely resistible offer."

Nonplussed, Annie fidgeted with her Frederick's of Hollywood brassiere in what I am sure she considered a most magnetic manner but which came across as a badly done scratching session.

"You ain't got a good head for bargains," she replied. "I could teach you a thing or two that them university girls ain't never thought of, much less ever done."

"Yes, I am sure you could, and in the process you would also provide me free of additional charge with a dose of microbes and bacteria that would confound the University of Georgia Infirmary for years. No, thanks."

Annie's ego was Kevlar-clad, for none of my rejections ever seemed to penetrate. Nevertheless, she shrugged off my obvious disinterest in her corporeal charms and went for the main chance.

"I guess you heard about me bein' in th' weddin'," she coyly observed.

Somewhat taken aback, I could only respond with the obvious—"Not yours, I hope."

"Well, no," she replied. "My family ain't much for gettin' married, if you catch my drift."

I caught. On a previous occasion she had tossed a ragged billfold onto Bubba's bar and had extracted a series of dog-eared photos of her family. Four generations of shifty-eyed males and slatternly females all looked suspiciously like her long-lived Great-Uncle Charlie, who in every picture was casting a lustful eye at the nearest daughter or niece. I ventured that Annie's ability to run fast had kept her from producing one of Great-Uncle Charlie's pointy-headed, fifth-generation offspring, and she had not denied the possibility.

"Thank God, he caught a minié ball in the leg during the Spanish-American War, or I never would have kept out of his grip!" she confided.

"So," I responded with reckless bravado, "if it weren't you or any of your thoroughly inbred clan who got hitched, then how did you get mixed up in a wedding ceremony?"

I should have known better. Annie was wound up with a tale that had to be related, and I had heard too many of her usually preposterous anecdotes not to have sensed the oncoming avalanche of mind-pickling events. Having opened myself for the full blast of Annie's rhetoric, I made a mental note that for future protection I should enroll in an ESP course.

"I was a bridesmaid," Annie said with great pride. "I got to march down the aisle and all that stuff. It was great!"

I tried to picture just who in the vast region of wiregrass Georgia would have the monumental effrontery, the ultissimo in bad taste to make Pulpwood Annie a part of the wedding party. My imagination failed me utterly, leaving me no recourse but to ask.

"Oh, it was the weddin' between Olga Turnipseed and Ramses Jones. I met her through the groom."

Much became blindly clear. Both of the nuptially inclined had been in my high school class. Olga was the kind of tall, rangy girl who would make Olive Oyle look absolutely curvaceous by comparison. Her mother had literary aspirations limited to reading an occasional racy novel, and she had chosen Olga's name after completing half a dozen pages of some obscure, lascivious Russian work. Mrs. Turnipseed later heard that "Olga" was Slavic for "ugly but distinctive," making it a most prescient choice.

As for Ramses, he was a thick-skulled mass of protoplasm on the large side of huge. Rumor at school had it he was named for a brand of prophylactic that failed, allowing one of his father's less lethargic sperm to slither through and assault his mother's egg sometime shortly after a Wednesday evening prayer meeting.

I couldn't think of a better-paired twosome. At least by having them linked in wedlock, it would prevent other people from making two of the worst choices of their lives. There is a God in Heaven after all.

However, I did not quite see the connection between Annie and Olga. So, foolish me, I just had to ask.

"I guess you could say it started out as sort of a mistake," Annie said in what was obviously an evasive effort.

"Go on."

I was relentless. My head was beginning to throb, a sure sign

Annie was beginning to get to me, or that the oxygen level was beginning to be depleted in Bubba's Bar by cigarette smoke and Hoyt's cologne. Whatever. I sensed a disgustingly delicious discourse that I knew I could not resist. Even if it hurt.

"Well," Annie continued, "it all began one night when Ramses and me was doin' it doggie fashion at the back of his pickup. Olga just happened to drive up, and Ramses made up a story, real quick, saying I was helpin' him push off the truck because it had a dead battery. It was pretty dark, and Ramses got his pants up real quick, and I guess she bought the whole thing. Olga said she appreciated my assistin' him so much she insisted on gettin' friendly. One thing led to another, and when she and Ramses got engaged, she axed me to be in the weddin'."

Annie dropped her eyes and executed what for her passed as a blush. "I appreciated the invite so much that I later reimbursed Ramses for the trick," she added.

How could anyone, even a dim bulb like Olga, confuse blatant sexual intercourse via the "patio entry" instead of the "front door" with shoving a stalled truck? Yet, why was I not too surprised at this revelation? Even so, why did it take a full minute for me to get the logical portion of my brain rehoused in order to digest this phenomenon before posing another question? But I digress.

"Okay," I said, "where and when did this wedding take place?"

Annie's eyes lit up with excitement. She reached into her purse, a plastic lizard skin lookalike she probably found at a dime store bargain counter, and fished out a pack of Lucky Strikes. She put one of the straighter ones between her carmine lips and lit it. The smoke disappeared quickly into a bronze haze that lurked just below the slowly oscillating blades of Bubba's sole form of air conditioning—squeaky ceiling fans.

"It was last week. They held it at the family church over in your county. It's located down one of them dirt roads. Sort of a ratty, badly painted wooden thing with a steeple that looked like it had been hit by lightnin' or something bad. I think they call it the First Holy Apostolic Church of the Miracle Pine Tree."

"Say again? Church of the Miracle what?" There are all sorts of weirdly named and strange-functioning religious groups metamorphosing throughout the South, but this was a new one for me.

"Well, they call it the Miracle Pine Tree. Olga said it was because a turpentine hand claimed that after he chipped a new 'face' on a big ole pine tree that it looked like Jesus. Then, all that tree sap started oozing out like He was wearin' a crown of thorns and was bleedin'. Folks out there considered it a sign. Built a church right on the spot."

"At least they didn't get snake handling mixed in," I added.

"Maybe they did," Annie replied. "Olga said one of them turpentine hands claimed he found a baby diamondback curled up in the sap cup just below Jesus. Said it looked like the snake was praying. Whadda ya think of that?"

"I think that snake was stuck in the sap. I think I had rather have a beer. I think I would rather be at Daytona Beach getting blasted with a certain sorority girl who would put out with a dead man. I think I would rather hear about your wedding experience."

As refuge, I emptied my Miller and quickly called for another. Never one to pass up an opportunity, Annie doubled the order and with an experienced nod of her head made clear to Bubba it was I who would manipulate the tab.

Then, an Edward R. Morrow-like furrow creased Annie's brow. Metaphorically, I girded my loins and prepared for what was to come. I felt strange tinglings in my prefrontal lobe, just below my fourth rib on the right side and in my left kneecap—formidable omens.

"Actually, it wasn't what I would call a real perfect weddin'", she said.

"Considering who the bride and groom were, I would say that was a foregone conclusion," I added acidly. "Weren't the church doors tall enough for Olga to enter without bending to the waist? Couldn't Ramses wriggle through without getting stuck?"

"It wasn't things like that," Annie said defensively. "It was more like, well, the unexpected things, if you catch my drift."

"For instance?"

"For instance, the candles. They had all them tall candles fastened to the sides of the pews, and they lit them before the crowd came in. It was a hot day, and them burning candles began to wilt and bend. They dripped hot wax all over anybody sittin' near them, and one extra-large blob dripped right down the front of this big ole woman wearing a low-cut dress. Talk about creatin' a sensation! You'd have thought it was a Holy Roller convention in full gear!"

Annie paused to eject a Lucky Strike cloud of cancer-triggering elements for whatever unfortunate patrons were foolishly trying to ingest some air inside Bubba's deathtrap den.

"Fortunately, the ushers got her out of the church before she turned over more than three pews. And there was folks sittin' in them pews at the time! And the language that woman used! I ain't never heard it that bad at Bubba's although some of the talk down at the Green Grotto on Saturday nights would run a close second sometimes!"

"Okay, you had the dripping tapers. And the scalded fat lady. And all those Holy Pine Tree worshippers upended ass over elbows in the pews. What else happened?"

I knew enough about Pulpwood Annie stories to disbelieve the possibility that this one would end in such a relatively tame manner.

"Like I said, it was them candles. They was all over the place. Burning like prime real estate in Hades. Olga and Ramses made it in and got down to where the minister was. That preacher, he was one of them leather-lung, shoutin' types who said the betrothed needed to be prayed over, and he launched into a real stemwinder. Well, there was this soloist standin' in the choir stall hidden by some greenery and a tier of candles. All of a sudden, them candles tilted over and set the greenery afire. Luckily, one of the ushers had his eyes open during the prayer and saw what was happenin'. He took off his coat quick as a wink and beat out the fire before that preacher finished his prayer! And just before that soloist got ignited!"

Annie paused to reflect on the cherished moment, then continued.

"Fortunately, the soloist was only singed a little bit and got off her song pretty well. Choked only once or twice on the smoke smoulderin' from the burned-out greenery."

At this point, all of my warning signs were moving from Condition Yellow to Condition Red. Steeped in logic, fairness and a Southern Baptist tolerance for most things not particularly fun, I knew I was hearing far more than my mental constitution was capable of processing. Annie was doing it again. Why didn't I ever learn?

The problem was I had too vivid an imagination. When Annie would get into the midst of one of her screwball, implausible stories like this one, I inexorably projected myself there, also. The only difference was that while my psyche was rebelling and rejecting the reality of her description and hitting the panic button, seeking the nearest exit, Annie was seeing all of the action as within her realm of normality. While I was breaking into a cold sweat, she was cucumber-like with calmness.

"My God, Annie, how terrible! Even for such miscreants as Olga and Ramses! Surely things calmed down after that. Tell me nothing else crazy happened!"

Annie paused and scrutinized me carefully. I like to think she took my measure and decided I was geared for The Big Picture.

"Actually, the ceremony continued pretty much as planned. Except at the end. That preacher shore loved to pray, and after he had pronounced them man and wife, he held up both his hands and began blessing them with a final prayer. That was my cue to kneel down and pick up the train on Olga's weddin'dress. Then, I was to follow them up the aisle. Nothing could have been simpler."

"And?"

"And, I did just as I was instructed. Soon as he began to pray, I knelt down. 'Course, I kept my eyes closed like I was supposed to during a prayer. Well, when the preacher finished up with a big A-MEN, I opened my eyes and reached for the train. Guess what? That Olga had already turned and was halfway up the aisle with Ramses!"

A gleam of anger flashed quickly across Annie's face.

"Oh, great! What'd you do?"

"You really don't want to know."

"Go ahead. Make my day."

"Well, there I was, on my knees in front of the whole wedding party. Guess it got the better of me. I jumped to my feet, said a big God-Damn-Son-of-a-Bitch just as loud as you please, stomped up the aisle and out of the church! Didn't slow down 'til I hit the blacktop. Hitched a ride back to Bubba's and drank a snootfull."

"Can't say I blame you a bit," I commiserated. "At least you tried, and you helped get Olga and Ramses married. That counts for something, doesn't it?"

Annie turned to me and blew a billow of smoke right at me.

"No, it don't count a pile of cow plop. During the honeymoon at Silver Springs, that Ramses ran off with one of them mermaids who put on a show there. Left Olga stuck at the motel with the bill and everything!

"All in all, it taught me a good lesson," Annie added with conviction.

"What's that?" I inquired.

"That my family's way is better. At least it's predictable. After all, when the same family members keep on reproducin' themselves, you can at least pretty well tell what to expect. No more weddin's for me."

And with that Annie hopped off the barstool, plucked a coin from her Frederick's of Hollywood brassiere, popped it into the jukebox and began freaking out to Willie Nelson.

I wish there was more, but that's all she told me. And guess what else? She never mentioned her last name.

Chapter 9

Pulpwood Annie and the Bootlegger

Just when Pulpwood Annie got involved with A.C. Peacock is lost in the lies and obfuscations of south Georgia mythology. Like halitosis and warts, A.C. kept popping into Annie's life on the most unexpected occasions, but considering Annie's line of work and her catholic disregard for her clients' appearance, odor, prison record, tattoos or lack of teeth, she was hardly in a position to consider A.C. as anything more than a typical cash-on-the-barrelhead customer.

Yet, when A.C. was in town, he was regular as rain in seeking out Annie, and I heard many a reference to him as I straddled an uncomfortable stool at Bubba's—always accompanied by Her Ribald Raunchiness. That A.C. Peacock was one of the area's biggest bootleggers meant he spent an inordinate amount of time in the brambles and thickets where he kept his still churning out rotgut white lightning. When not distilling, A.C. was hauling this insalubrious fluid to Savannah, Brunswick and Jacksonville to sell to poor whites and coloreds who could not afford or who had not developed a taste for bonded whiskey.

Scarcely a poster child for the public health department, A.C. was nonetheless the possessor of a fancy car and plenty of money. He also had a distinctly diminished sense of feminine quality and style, being as he often turned to Annie for his lustful lunges.

But who can explain taste? All one has to do is drive through any south Georgia county to observe worn-out Jim Walter houses and rusty trailers situated on sagging, soggy lots, in miasmic swamps and/

or surrounded by rattlesnake-infested palmetto clumps. Such sites are usually garnished with refrigerators and washing machines on the front porches and rusty old trucks and dismantled cars scattered around the perimeter. So, why expect the likes of A.C. Peacock to move higher up the coital chain than Annie? However, I digress.

When he was in town—an event that usually coincided with the county sheriff's taking his family to St. Simons Island for a swim in the sea—A.C. would slink into Zenobia and scurry over to Bubba's or wherever Annie happened to be in business.

"Can't really say there was anything special about A.C.," Annie casually observed one evening after having conned me into investing several quarters in the juke box to hear an unending round of Kitty Wells's latest anthems. She also got me for several rounds of Miller High Life.

"'Cept, he shore pissed off his wife with his runnin' around with me," she added almost as an afterthought.

Considering that Annie had done it with more married men than Carter has Little Liver Pills, this did not come across as front-page news. On the other hand, Annie's stories of late had been rather drab and predictable, and there was the possibility that this new episode would be so tantalizingly trashy and incommodious to community standards that I would tingle lasciviously as I recalled each X-rated detail.

"So, what happened?" I breathlessly murmured.

That's all it took.

Seems that A.C.'s one touch of class involved his disinclination to connect with Annie in the back seat of his car, at the scummy Honeysuckle Motel or on the Zenobia Lover's Lane, which doubled as a lumpy, condom-littered detour to the county dump.

Instead, he got to taking her to his fishing cabin located on one of the less-overgrown branches of Big Satilla Creek. Constructed of grade-Z pine boards and decorated in early wiregrass Georgia castoffs and army surplus equipment, the cabin reeked of kerosene lamps, long-departed catfish, sweaty maleness and bay rum—A.C.'s unimaginative substitute for soap, water and deodorant. Of course,

Annie loved it, as would anybody who had morphed through untold months of the fetid, cut-'em-with-a-knife vapors drifting constantly about in Bubba's place.

"We tried doin' it on an ol' army cot," Annie revealed in a Dolby Sound-like whisper. "It squeaked and squawked and then just plain collapsed. So, we got ourselves untangled and continued on the floor. Ended up with my butt full of pine splinters, too!"

"My, my," I observed. "I thought you would have used one of A.C.'s pre-Civil War army blankets to cushion your workplace."

Annie snorted in derision.

"Not me! Them blankets A.C. keeps in that cabin is so dirty I wouldn't wrap a hound dog in one! Much less me!"

Well! The fastidious Annie! Will miracles never cease? However, this conversation was fast meandering into the uninteresting minutiae of Annie's life. I had to get the story back on track immediately.

"Now, Annie, you're drifting. What about that reference you just made about A.C's wife? Not that having south Georgia female spouses angry at you is any great shakes," I said.

Annie paused to swig a healthy portion of the Miller sitting before her. Then, she extended her badly tattooed and occasionally bruised arms straight up and let forth with a mighty yawn that would have been marginally dignified if she had kept her mouth closed. Having conducted her aerobic exercise for the day, she refocused her squinty, red-rimmed eyes on me and continued.

"I'll jes' tell you what A.C. filled me in on later. Seems that his wife, Vera, was gettin' pretty tired of A.C.'s messin' around with honky-tonk pickups, whores and the like. She had to be disinfected at the health office for a few rounds of crabs that he brought home, and she claimed she'd had too many close calls with false positive reports on the clap to put up with any more from A.C."

Sounded like A.C. was the Typhoid Mary of social diseases in these parts. I later pondered on the absence of Annie's concern about these undesirable infections. Maybe she had built up immunity. Leave it to Annie to be spirochete-resistant.

The sordid story continued pretty much to form. Seems Vera got wind of A.C.'s using the fishing cabin for his trysts, so she enlisted the help of her children—Evie and Ayres—to lay a trap. As luck would have it, Annie was the additional figure in this pineywoods ménage a trois.

Apparently, Vera's plan was to burst into the cabin at a particularly sensitive moment and loudly harangue A.C. and female friend while Ayers took photos with a flashbulb camera and Evie operated a somewhat bulky, battery-powered tape recorder. Indisputable blackmail, if not prime evidence for alimony, lay behind this scheme.

It is one thing to dream up the perfect ambush. It is another to pull it off without a hitch. Alas, in misbegotten marriages as well as in other aspects of daily living, there is always one more thing to ponder that does not get thought about in time.

Such was the case here, and Annie fairly glowed with excitement as she got into the meat of the story.

"As usual when I went to the cabin with A.C., we had a few drinks from his still. In fack, he had a load of the stuff he was gettin' ready to take down to Savannah. We had the pick of the litter, so to speak," she said. "My! That 'shine was good, and before long we was feelin' mighty friendly towards each other! I was just hangin' my new Frederick's of Hollywood dress on a nail when all hell broke loose!"

The morality patrol of Vera, Evie and Ayers—along with their assorted evidentiary equipment—came roaring through the cabin door. In the excitement, complicated and confused in large part because of Vera's eardrum-shattering imprecations and shrieks—Ayres fumbled with the flashbulb camera and managed to take several exciting close-ups of his left thumb and of his right nostril. Partly blinded by that last shot, he careened into Evie, causing her to hit the "fast forward record" switch on the tape machine. The end result of this blunder was a fascinating transcription done at warp speed, a typical portion being something like, "YoucheatingsonovabitchIfinallygotthegoodsonyouNowVerait ain'twhatitseemsGoodGodamightylookatDaddyIhadnoideahewas hunglikethatHeydon'ttouchmydressit'snew!!"

As one can imagine, the offended Peacocks were less than prepared to go before the Supreme Court with lead-pipe-cinch-proof of A.C.'s adultery.

Despite the early setback to their plans, the vengeance-seeking trio regrouped quickly and began attacking poor A.C. While he manfully and unsuccessfully sought to counter verbal and physical blows, slaps, badly aimed projectiles of spit and a few well-aimed thrusts to the groin area, he did not see Annie retrieving her Frederick's of Hollywood dress and sneaking out the door.

"Last I saw of the mess, they had A.C. on the floor and was tyin' him up with a clothesline rope," she said. "I heard later they was gonna keep him hogtied in that cabin forever, but they didn't count on reinforcements!"

Hey! This was shaping up to be one of Annie's better yarns. Reinforcements! Visions of spear-filled battles on the plains of Troy, black-hulled ships, sulky demi-gods, treacherous immortals and the wine-dark sea flashed across my stimulated brain.

Unlike *The Iliad*, it was not Rumor that ran rampant amongst the troops. Instead, it was Hector Bryan, A.C.'s right-hand man at the still. Hector had a habit of sticking pretty close to A.C. in case somebody tried to arrest him or to steal his load. Wearing bib overalls and a battered straw hat, he was snoozing under a nearby sycamore tree, waiting until A.C. had finished balling Annie, when the sounds of pitched battle flickered into his cauliflowered ears.

Hector was on his feet in an instant and was moving as rapidly as a three-hundred-pound former fullback can toward the noisy cabin. He burst through the door, saw the naked A.C. roped fore and aft and began to clean house.

Out of a window went the camera and Ayers, who managed a great wing shot of Hector's enraged face before Ayers crashed into the Big Satilla Creek shallows. Vera received a severe field-goal-like punt in the derriere, which sent her zooming into the bathroom. After bouncing off the grimy commode, she flopped backward into the tub and sank into blissful unconsciousness.

As for Evie, she received what almost passed for her first sexual experience when Hector stumbled after booting Vera and fell forward onto her, crushing Evie down onto the collapsed army cot. After several unsuccessful shoves, rolls and thrusts, the beefy Hector managed to stagger to his feet, leaving the semi-squashed Evie in a swoon, convinced she had been penetrated, although it was only a strategically situated wooden leg from the broken cot that the girl took for her phallic encounter.

"So, what happened next?" I quickly inquired.

For reasons I never understood, denouements that would leave an ordinary person gasping in disbelief or amazement usually left Annie completely nonplussed. She took a dainty swig from her can of Millers and cast an experienced eye over the crowd to see who else might be listening. Satisfied with whatever she saw, she continued.

"It was real simple. I tossed my dress in the back seat of A.C.'s car, cranked that sucker up and hightailed it back to my trailer in Zenobia. Figgered I would return the car to A.C. later," she said.

"That's it?"

"Well, no."

"And…?"

Annie looked flustered and, if possible, a mite embarrassed.

"It's like this, and don't you tell nobody. I usually collect my fee in advance, even from an old reliable like A.C. But we got to nippin' that 'shine, and I plumb forgot to collect! Realized I was shy soon as I parked his car at the trailer.

"Then, I remembered that load of hooch he had in the trunk. Decided I would take that in trade. Especially since his crazy family pert-near scared me to death back at the cabin when they came a-bustin' in like that!"

The ever-resourceful Annie had proceeded to unload the entire cargo—some fifty quarts. She then repacked those Mason jars full of liquid dynamite in some innocent-looking Southern Bread cardboard boxes and stacked them in the back of her pickup truck. I know because she dragged me into the parking lot to check out her haul.

"Here, have a sample," she proffered, poking one of the toxicogenic jars in my direction.

"Not a chance," I said with more determination that I could usually muster around an Annie offer. "That concoction of radiator drippings, raccoon poop and lead salts would shrivel my manhood into negative space and blow a hole the size of a billiard ball through the top of my head! Save it for your enemies!"

Annie shrugged off my less-than-complimentary critique of her cache.

"Now that it's the weekend, I guess I'll jes' have to drive this load down to Savannah myself," she said. "Figger I can sell most of it to the whores and hangers-on down along River Street. Maybe Indian Lil or one of them other workin' girls over there can put me on to some buyers. I'll return A.C.'s car when I get back. Wanna come along?"

I could not decide which was more dangerous: riding to Savannah in her beat-up International-Harvester truck or running the risk of getting arrested by the GBI for moonshining. Besides, I had my hands full of dealing with Annie on any given evening in Zenobia. What if Indian Lil took a fancy to me when I was in the sovereign state of Chatham?

"I disincline on the grounds it would incriminate me," I managed a weak reply.

"Phooey! I been incriminatin' myself for years with nary an arrest for nothin'," she boasted. "But, if you ain't up to it, you ain't up to it. Bye!"

Away went Annie, bound for Georgia's First City and what I am sure would be a baker's dozen assorted adventures between there and back. Thank God, I had managed to avoid that veritable Custer's Last Stand. On the other hand, being Annie, she would be back in Zenobia before long with money and stories to tell. I made a note not to come over until this latest set of events had faded into the froth of her other fabled adventures. But then, if I did that, I would again miss the chance of finding out Annie's last name.

Chapter 10

Pulpwood Annie and the Diamond Ring

Considering Pulpwood Annie's predilection for one-night stands as income and incest for keeping the family genes within easy reach, it came as a shock when I learned she was doing traffic with Vance Roper. He provided neither.

South Georgia's gift to wholesale whoring, that proverbial Blue Light Special of cheapie sex in all its unrewarding scents, sights, inferences and connotations, Pulpwood Annie was constitutionally disinclined to give away that for which she charged so little. At the same time, Vance was of that breed of honky-tonk hangers-on who never paid for sex that he could get for free.

As usual, I was on weekend furlough from Bulldog Heaven, the University of Georgia, and I was wetting my whistle at Bubba's Bar in Zenobia when I first learned about the unusual congress between Annie and Vance. Both were notorious within Bubba's sweaty, smoky environs. Annie had been hustling drinks and two-dollar-a-pop sex there since Moses led the Children of Israel from mighty Egypt. Or so it seemed to me. On the other hand, Vance was a parvenu who preyed on any woman capable of going horizontal, who considered his superficially flashy allure to be the universal coin of the realm and who could stomach his appearance and corpse-like personality.

Yes, Vance Roper was a package of goods. He drove a big, red Cadillac El Dorado convertible and displayed a Michigan bankroll at every opportunity. He drank expensive whiskey, bet large sums on his billiard skills and was famous for his willingness to cold-cock an irascible rival, usually when the unsuspecting fellow was three sheets to the wind and looking the other way.

Vance's father, Sam, gained fame during World War II by successfully avoiding the draft. He did this by getting a deferment in order to manufacture wooden stocks for M-1 rifles. This patriotic and quite lucrative venture began December 8, 1941, when Sam realized his ass was cannon fodder if he didn't do something quick. A call to his congressman got Sam a contract for the rifle stocks, and the rest is history. He became Zenobia's first millionaire. A renewable chunk of that money inevitably ended up in the hands of his son, Vance.

Whereas Sam was tall, slim and handsome with dark, curly locks, heavily lidded eyes and a smile that would have given a tarantula second thoughts, his offspring turned out to be short, pudgy and balding. The scion also possessed the sex appeal akin to a bad case of prickly heat. Nature's compensation, however, was Vance's cash. It smelt of power and privilege and all of the seven deadly sins, and as a result the youth was seldom lonely.

Company is one thing. Permanent companionship is another. Maybe Sam Roper had begun to sense the Grim Reaper's approach; at any rate, he accelerated his demands that Vance produce an heir to carry on the manufacturing empire.

I must say that Vance tried. Word has it he proposed to every eligible white girl within a day's drive of Zenobia. Alas, while Vance provided ample entertainment, food and drink for his dates, his Piltdown Man presence and zero-minus personality tended to counteract the magnetic attraction that money usually had upon the female psyche. In short, he courted many, proposed to all and got turned down every time. The two-carat diamond engagement ring he carried with him everywhere had more disparate fingerprints on it than a Port-A-Potty door handle at a south Georgia barbecue.

Cynics claimed Vance was like a highway patrol officer—he had a certain minimum number of proposals he had to proffer each day in order to meet his expected quota. As a result, the more sensitive maidens took to running, ducking into alleys or hiding behind store counters when they saw Vance approaching. It was really that bad.

Which explains, I suppose, why Vance took to hanging out at Bubba's and inevitably ended up within Pulpwood Annie's orbit. Any port in a storm, Vance obviously reasoned, and from a gynecological point of view, Annie certainly qualified as being of the female gender. The problem was Annie insisted upon charging for her services, whereas Vance refused to pay for something he considered like the air and the ocean—open and free for all.

Vance began carting Annie around in his red El Dorado. He took her over to Waycross to eat at the Green Frog Restaurant, which at that time was pineywood Georgia's gastronomical equivalent to The Four Seasons. They water-skied at nearby Johnson's Lake, swam at Jay Bird Springs and even picnicked near the abandoned Coast Guard station on St. Simons Island.

Whoever said romance has its own set of problems obviously had Vance and Annie in mind. Annie was accustomed to boorish, clumsy, profane, smelly clients, but they all possessed one unique virtue—they paid before having gotten gratification. Vance wanted to connect, he wanted to marry in order to get Sam Roper off his fat little back, but he down and out refused to pay a penny in order to penetrate Annie.

Once, while cadging a Miller from me at Bubba's, she told me that she had had her palm greased every time a man lunged her way, even going back to her fabled deflowering by a brother when she was barely a teenager and for which she earned a quarter.

"I don't care if Vance's got a pocket full of rings, I ain't comin' across for him 'til he pays for it," she snorted defiantly. "It's a matter of family pride and tradition!"

"But, Annie," I protested, "if you marry him, you won't have to charge anybody again for your services!"

That went over about as successfully as somebody suggesting that the Pope enter into matrimony with Mother Teresa.

And so the stalemate continued. Vance saw in Annie his last, best hope for matrimony and the cessation of continual harangues from his rich but obsessed father. Annie saw economic potential in Vance but was having difficulty figuring out a way to squeeze a few dollars from him in exchange for sex.

Ah, but the loom of love weaves many a pattern in the cloth of courtship.

A philosopher would compare Annie and Vance to the concept of the irresistible force encountering the immovable object. In science, this situation remains locked forever in some kind of metaphysical morass. Not so with us humans. Flesh, fortunately, has a yielding point. And so it was that one day after their usual go-around on who had to do what in order for the other to do something else, Vance made what he considered to be The Big Compromise.

Taking the engagement ring from his pocket, he rubbed it briskly on the seat of his dungarees—no doubt a Freudian gesture to wipe out the bitter memory of all those rejections, if not all those fingerprints—thrust it onto one of Annie's less nicotine-stained fingers and muttered what he considered to be the clinching words:

"Take the damn thing, Annie! If you marry me like I want you to, I'll start givin' you an allowance. You can pretend it's your usual fee!"

Swelling in pride at his idea, Vance assumed a pose suggesting he was the first to coin the concept of quid pro quo.

Annie was rarely at a loss for words, but something deep inside the most primitive level of her cerebrum suggested she stall for time in order to think things over. She got out her dime-store-purchased Maybelline compact and proceeded to powder every patch of unexposed skin or hair follicle on her face. Then, she began rearranging her Frederick's of Hollywood chemise, a tight little number with three glow-in-the-dark hands imprinted strategically across the front.

"Well, I don't know," she said, while all the time eyeing the sparkler on her bony digit. "Don't seem like it's quite the same thing. What if we don't do it for a week? Do I still get the allowance?"

The desperate Vance decided to consider that a rhetorical question that could await some future consideration. He dropped Annie off at Bubba's as quickly as possible and floorboarded the El Dorado as he pointed its grinning grill toward home. The reason for such haste was to inform his father with the happy news.

The dim-witted Vance was ill prepared for Sam's response.

"What?! You can't marry that ol' whore," shouted the sire. "Great Godamighty! Every man-jack in the county has had her, including me a few times, when your mother was on the rag or pissed off about something!"

Nonplussed, Vance defended his action as best he could.

"Well, you said you wanted me to get married and have a bunch of kids. I been trying. I been turned down by pert-near every white woman between here and Macon. I finally get one to agree, and you raise hell about it. You don't like my choice, go find a wife for me!"

And with that, Vance stalked out of the room.

However, Vance solved his problem the next time he stopped by at Mom's Diner in Zenobia, for he spotted a cute little red-haired waitress slinging hash. Vance turned on the charm and convinced the girl that he was the man of her dreams. The fact that she was easily approachable and extremely nearsighted aided Vance greatly in this endeavor. The clincher came when Vance said he wanted the girl to meet his folks.

No sooner said than done. Tiffany Odum soon found herself the houseguest of Zenobia's wealthiest man. Although somewhat startled by the vague hunk looming before her, she bravely began chatting with Vance, and soon the two were, by Sam's eagle-eyed standards, getting along famously. In short order they were engaged. Vance ran down to the jewelry store and bought another large, expensive ring, for both he and Sam had written off the one Vance had so unwisely given Annie.

Of course, Annie soon learned all about the revised wedding plans. Being somewhat philosophical about the whole matter, and considering that her lifestyle usually supplied events far more supercharged and stimulating than being left waiting at the church house steps, she shrugged it off.

"It ain't as though I was burnin' to get hitched," she confided to me one evening during a Miller chug-a-lug contest I had initiated with her. "I'd uv give him back the ring if he'd bothered to come around and axed for it."

I admired that sentiment so much that I ordered us another six-pack.

The Annie-Vance-Tiffany situation quickly faded from the public mind after the Ropers threw a mammoth wedding and a reception that drenched Zenobia's elite with champagne and enough brie on Ritz crackers to cause an epidemic of indigestion and diarrhea. However, tongues wagged for weeks about the nerve of Sam Roper, serving alcohol in the Methodist church recreation room! Others, smitten by the alien brie, muttered that in the future they were swearing off all forms of cheese except for cheddar.

Unfortunately, the marriage of Vance and Tiffany did not last long enough for the yahoos at the barbershop to lay bets as to when it would disintegrate. Tiffany took a fancy to Vance's red Cadillac El Dorado and began driving it around town. The nearsighted girl obviously did not see an ancient oak tree growing in front of the courthouse, and she plowed right into it, smashing the convertible into a seemingly irreparable mess.

Tiffany escaped serious injury, but a blow to the head when she hit the steering wheel and the general shaking up she experienced must have activated a hitherto unused portion of her reasoning process. At any rate, she suddenly saw Vance for what he was, and, even worse for Vance, for what he decidedly was not, and she left him flat. Tiffany moved immediately back to her home in Valdosta, where her mother consoled her daughter by directing her to the most avaricious divorce lawyer in Georgia.

On my next trip to Zenobia and Bubba's, I encountered Annie. She was perched on a barstool, blowing smoke rings into the already carcinogen-laden Celotex ceiling. Never one to shy away from another person's pain, I asked her if she had heard about Vance and Tiffany.

"Yeah," she replied laconically.

"Well, what do you think about it?"

"Coulda told that red-haired girl it wouldn't work. Wouldn't have done no good, though. And I wasn't exactly the kind of person she was gonna run into for a chat."

I couldn't resist rubbing salt into a potential wound.

"What about Vance?"

Annie brightened, scratched a furry underarm and daintily dropped her cigarette into my beer.

"He's okay. I fixed him up!"

I was transfixed.

"What? You finally hit the sack with Vance? How? When? How much did you charge him?"

Annie gave me her best what-rock-did-you-just-crawl-out-from-under look.

"That ain't it at all," she replied archly.

"Then what do you mean? Curious minds want to know."

"I'm gonna give him back his car."

"What car? His car was wrecked. I saw it."

Annie was now in her element. She had my undivided attention, and she was about to hit me with a denouement that I would neither anticipate nor understand.

"That's about what I'd uv expected from a know-it-all college smart aleck like you! I bet you couldn't plug a lamp socket into the wall, much less repair a busted-up car. Well, I know a feller or two who can. What I did was go out to the junkyard and buy that beat-up Cadillac. Had it towed to the Chevy place and put my contacts to work. Took 'em three weeks to do it, but they got every part back in place. Spray-painted it real nice, too!"

I was staggered.

"But Annie, how did you do this? It must have cost a small fortune."

"I hocked the ring. C'mon, I got the car parked out back. You oughtta see it!"

I fell in line behind her as she sashayed behind the counter, through what passed for Bubba's kitchen and out the rear door.

And there it sat, gleaming in the sun. It was the Cadillac El Dorado, top down, red as original sin and looking for all the world like God's own roadster come down from the clouds.

"I figgered I owed Vance at least this," Annie said. "If he was desperate enough to propose to a tramp like me, then I guess I hadda do something for him when he was draggin' anchor."

She got into the car, cranked it and popped the gear into reverse.

"Gonna deliver it to him right now. Want to come?"

"No. This is your hour. Your show. Go to it."

And with that, Annie backed fiercely away from the building, threw the gear into drive, hit the gas and disappeared with the wave of a nicotine-ravaged hand.

In fact, she left so quickly I didn't have time to compliment her on her gallant gesture. And, as usual, I forgot to ask her about her last name.

Chapter 11

How She Affected Dewey's Decimal System

About the only time Pulpwood Annie came near the Zenobia Public Library was once when her pickup broke down in front of it, and she had to stand on the porch to avoid the rain while waiting for the Chevy place to send out a tow truck. Which is not big news, for it was only the crčme de la crčme of Zenobian society who had either the reading skills or the discretionary time to plow through its world-class collection of Sidney Shelton, Barbara Cartland, Danielle Steele and Jacqueline Susann novels.

In fact, to associate Annie with the library was to create a contradiction in terms, for the two Zenobian institutions were poles apart in mutual need and interest. It remains one of those imponderable coincidences of which history is replete that this is how she met Dewey DeWitt Swain, for he was driving the vehicle that arrived to rescue her beat-up International-Harvester truck.

Guess what ensued?

Yes, for seemingly endless hours thereafter, I was overwhelmed with Annian gush about Dewey's many charms, capacities and endurance between the sheets.

When given the choice between a legend and the truth, one had better lean toward the legend, for truth may be a bit saltier because it includes the downplayed shortcomings of the hero in question. Legend always carries with it the glow of generous generalities. And the afterglow of selected remembrances. Such would prove to be the case with Annie's latest conquest. The reader is forewarned.

My encounters with the fabled Dewey usually involved hearing him long before he came into sight. A classic blowhard, he possessed a drill sergeant's vocabulary that he projected in a stentorian, eardrum-piercing tenor reminiscent of Don Knotts in the throes of a panic attack. His aural image flew in the face of his physical one, for he was undoubtedly a handsome man. Dewey had a shock of bright red hair, regular facial features complemented by sideburns and a pencil-thin mustache. The usual clanking accumulation of K-Mart gold-plate jewelry hung around his bronzed neck and displayed glitteringly in his rusty- looking chest hair. His sartorial choice tended toward shiny black shirts and skin-tight jeans.

I had to admit Dewey was a fine figure of a man who was still into the full flush of virility. I also could see why Annie was constantly drooling over him. What got my goat was his constant one-upmanship on any topic that occurred among the cracker think-tank members who convened more or less regularly around the fringes of Bubba's Bar. If Fishbait Bailey had a new truck, Dewey had a bigger, shinier, faster one. If Barney Bullard owned a prize breeding boar, Dewey knew about one that had a higher sperm count. If Porter Shoemaker had scored mightily with the girls at Daytona Beach, Dewey had done twice as many who were twice as pretty and who charged half as much the last time he was in Miami. You get the picture.

I normally would have made the usual effort to move down room whenever Dewey was gusting forth, and I would probably have given him no more consideration than I did Annie's other two-dollar marks, if she just hadn't gotten a whiff of religion.

One of the few things that worked really well on Annie's rattletrap truck was the radio, and the Zenobia station blared continually from a beat-up speaker that threatened to shake loose and fall onto the truck floor. Among the mix of programs was a thirty-minute travesty featuring Sister Sophie Summerall, a self-anointed preacher of the Pentecostal persuasion. Sister Sophie specialized in a series of ecclesiastical snorts, exclamations, whoops and repetitious holy generalities that hypnotized the listener with her zeal, if not her theology. What her religious tenets were certainly remained a mystery to me, being as about the only intelligible words I ever heard through the static were GLO-O-r-e-e to GAOD!! HalleLEWyah!! Praise JAY-zus! He's comin' SOON!! Get ready to meet YORE PER-R-R-SONAL SAVEYER!! YAY-us!!

Captivated by the messages pouring daily from her dusty dash, Annie became obsessed with attending one of Sister Sophie's tent revivals when next it appeared on the outskirts of town, and she insisted I attend with her.

"Well, I've never been to one of the meetings, and it might do me a bit of good to have a little religion tossed my way," I bravely observed. "If it will get your mind off the carnal delights you are enjoying with Dewey Swain, it will be a night well spent."

Anytime Annie got enthusiastic about something, she went at it whole hog, and this made it obligatory that we get seats as close to the front of the tent as possible. She must have figured religion got absorbed by osmosis as well as by conviction. At any rate, we were so near the somewhat-elevated plywood stage that we saw and heard everything in microscopic detail and in stereophonic, wrap-around sound.

First, there was the obligatory offering and the usual lusty singing of several tried-and-true hymns, all accompanied by a tambourine-wielding, wild-eyed woman, a tubercular-looking piano player, what apparently were two parolees on guitars and a spaced-out youth whacking some drums. Then, the main event entered the tent and mounted the platform.

Wow! Sister Sophie was a knockout! She possessed a generous figure, a narrow waist, curly black hair, eyes that would nail a eunuch to the wall and legs one only dreamed about. She wore a dress of thin, electric blue material that swirled temptingly whenever she gestured or sashayed about on the stage. If this was modern religion, I had been missing out!

Like Dewey Swain, she didn't sound at all like she looked. It may have been her appearance that first raised doubts in Annie's mind about this icon that hitherto had resonated in her brain as some kind of perfection that should be emulated. I think Annie knew enough about women and women's wiles to read Sister Sophie's book rather quickly.

As soon as Sister Sophie started preaching, it became clear to me that the radio Sophie was nowhere like the person performing in front of me. She quickly acknowledged this, using a technique that has worked like a charm ever since Saul got struck blind on the road to Damascus. The sinner who sees The Light, literally or figuratively, has an irresistible story to tell, and the listeners have a delicious sin for which they can proffer forgiveness.

"My dear friends from radioland," Sister Sophie began melodramatically, "I stand before you tonight a new woman, cleansed of my one great sin. BLESS HIS HOLY NAME!!"

At this point, half the audience got out handkerchiefs and began sniffling and honking into them.

"What is my great sin?" she exclaimed while moving quickly about the stage, her skirt aswirl. "I will tell you! PRAISE JAY-ZUS!!"

At this point, the half of the audience not sobbing joyfully into their handkerchiefs leaned forward in rapt attention. The elderly cupped hands over their hound-dog-like ears to capture every sizzling syllable.

"I have been guilty of the terrible sin of false modesty! YAY-US!!" Sister Sophie shouted. "I was raised up in a God-fearing family that believed women should reject vain things and disguise their God-given charms! HE'S COMING SOON!!"

At this point, the air was filled with a host of male and female "amens!"

Sister Sophie continued. "I used to wear my hair uncut and up in a bun on the back of my head! I didn't wear makeup! I didn't use perfume! I made my own clothes and didn't wear revealing things! I didn't shave my legs! HALLE-LEW-YAH!!"

At this point, everybody began studying her legs.

"I didn't wear suggestive underwear! GLORY!!" she added with what I easily discerned as a twinkle in her eyes.

At this point, everybody began checking out her bosom, the

electric blue dress providing more than a discreet crack of cleavage.

"FALSE MODESTY! SELAH!!" she shouted.

At this point, the startled audience jumped in surprise.

"I have had a revelation!" Sister Sophie proclaimed in a voice that vibrated the walls of the canvas cathedral. "I ain't gonna do that no more! BLESSED BE TH' LAMB!!"

This started a low buzz as the audience began murmuring support for and distress about this exposé.

"I am a new woman in the Lord! Instead of wallerin' in the sin of false modesty, I now embrace those things once thought of as evil but which now I see are GOOD! I'm now going to preach the GOSPEL OF GOOD THINGS! I cut my hair and perm it with a Toni! YAY-US! I use lipstick and rouge! GLORY BE! I dab Orange Blossom perfume behind my ears! PRAISE HIM! I shop for dresses at the K-Mart! AMEN, AMEN!!"

Sister Sophie paused to gain the full impact of what would come next. She stepped to the edge of the stage and stood, her feet slightly apart, her electric blue dress twisting temptingly at the edges.

"And I shave my legs! FORGIVE THEM FATHER THEY KNOW NOT WHAT THEY DO!!" she loudly and somewhat confusingly concluded, although having made a point I had already observed with satisfaction.

The rest of the service was an in-depth expansion on the Gospel of Good Things message she had just proclaimed and how she was better prepared to preach the Word now that the awful burden of false modesty had been lifted from her. After a while, most of the audience got on board and amen-ed! Sister Sophie's every pronunciamento. I remained fascinated by my up-close view of her now-sinless cleavage and guilt-free gams.

The service concluded with Sister Sophie announcing that her transformation had no effect upon her being a Member of the Cloth, "only now I'm gonna be wearing silk instead of drip-dry cotton!" Then came the usual post-message offering and some enthusiastic healing as all the males who could make it to the altar came up to have Sister Sophie lay hands on them. I was tempted to respond but refrained because I knew I might be compelled to "lay hands" on her, too.

Annie was in a rush to leave. I gathered she had had enough religion for one night. In fact, she seemed a bit disgruntled.

"I ain't sure that woman's on the up-and-up!" she announced. "I shore had her pictured different on the radio!"

"Images can be deceiving. Don't go by what you see. Go by what you feel," I offered in my best Southern Baptist ministerial style.

"What you mean?"

"Well, Sister Sophie may draw more male attention and female jealousy than a pie on the window sill will attract ants, but that doesn't diminish what she had to say."

"Such as?"

"Meaning, do good. Lend a helping hand. Live for others. That sort of thing." I was amongst the theological rocks and rills at this point and hoped mightily I did not have to proceed any farther in what for me was the dead end of my religious convictions.

"Oh," Annie said.

How words spoken in desperation can come ricocheting back will be seen in what happened next.

At Bubba's, things quickly returned to normal. I continued to come over occasionally for a brew, and when I did, I more often than not saw and chatted with Annie if she was in between clients. She seemed happy and whatever passed for normal for her. That is, until the evening when I found her grinding her teeth in anger.

"It's what I get for listenin' to you!" she shot at me before I even had a chance to pony up a round of Millers.

"Wha? Wha?" was the best I could muster while under this blistering blitzkrieg attack.

"Lend a helpin' hand, you said! Look what it got me!" she snapped back.

Having battled more or less successfully with the razor-sharp minds of the University of Georgia faculty, I rallied quickly and responded in more than fractured syllables.

"What in the world are you talking about? Are you smoking funny cigarettes again? Could you have reached the tertiary stage of syphilitic infection?"

A few choice defamations regarding my sainted reputation mingled with the usual uproar at Bubba's before I managed to get some idea of what was burning her behind. After disentangling Annie's pungent syntax, I determined she had had some kind of problem with Dewey Swain, a difficulty for which I was the cause celebre.

Here's what happened.

Annie was so inspired by my interpretation of Sister Sophie's sermon that she became inspired to "lend a helping hand." The first hand she encountered was attached to that family reprobate, Great-Uncle Charlie. A freshet had washed out the rickety, one-lane wooden excuse for a bridge he had constructed to span the creek in front of his farmhouse. Now, he was having to drive his pickup on a fifty-mile loop to get to Zenobia for groceries and to service a portion of his women friends. His usually limited funds provided for little more than a rude patch-up job for the bridge—one that would probably last until the next heavy downpour.

"So, were you going out there, hammer in hand, to nail that bridge back into place?" I asked.

"Yeah, if it took that. But when I told Dewey about the washout, he upped and volunteered to do the job himself."

"Dewey Swain? The great engineer? He does good to back that wrecker of his close to a tow job and not into it."

"Not accordin' to Dewey. Said he had built all sorts of things, and that ol' bridge would be a snap!"

Far-seeing words!

I couldn't believe what I was hearing, so I continued to pepper Annie with piercing questions.

"You mean to tell me you gave Dewey the job without checking with anybody else first?"

"Naw, silly. I talked with ol' man Moody—you don't know him; he repairs all them wooden bridges that the county maintains. He was familiar with the one on Great-Uncle Charlie's property and give me a pretty good idea of what it would cost to restore it so's Great-Uncle Charlie could drive over it some more."

"Then, why wasn't old man Moody on the job?"

"'Cause I tole Dewey what ol' man Moody estimated, and Dewey said he could do the job quicker and for less, that's why!"

All became clear. That windbag, that blustering, blathering know-it-all had conned Annie into letting him repair the bridge.

"Okay. I gather the famous fashioner of chicken coops, hanger of screen doors and installer of wooden shelves was going to span the creek. What happened?"

Annie began to hem and haw, a clear signal to my Psychology 101-prepared mind that she was undergoing some level of embarrassment. I pressed on.

"Come on, tell the truth. Did Dewey actually hit a lick on that bridge?"

Seems that Dewey took quite seriously his hasty bid to rebuild the bridge. He ran down to the dime store and bought paper, a ruler, a compass and a few pencils. He spent hours at the lumber yard, talking board feet, tensile strength and price with the owner. He set up his "office" in Annie's trailer and began sketching and figuring just how to do it.

As Annie confessed to me, she had no idea how complicated it was to re-create a bridge, even one as ridiculous as Great-Uncle Charlie's ill-fated one. She began hanging around Dewey during his calculations, and inevitably she soon began talking, flirting, then propositioning. Dewey's manhood could stand just so much, and he spent as much time entertaining himself with Annie as he did entertaining ideas for the bridge. The wastepaper basket overflowed with fantasy sketches and badly summed arithmetical calculations as Dewey's brain fought a losing battle between engineering and carnal release.

Finally, Dewey announced he had the design figured out. He went to the lumber yard, ordered what his measurements determined he needed, had it delivered to the creek bank and began assembling his creation.

All this took time, and Annie kept me informed with breathless up-to-date reports. Once Dewey actually started work on the bridge, she insisted I accompany her out there to see it. I went and was surprised. It actually looked like a bridge. The supporting spans met the creek bank at a safe angle and rested on sturdy beams sunk into mid-creek. A layer of two-by-fours carpeted the spans, and two rows of parallel one-by-sixes served as tracks a car or truck should follow.

I was impressed and insisted that I be permitted to view the final product when the first vehicle crossed over.

The big day finally arrived, and a crowd of Great-Uncle Charlie's children, grandchildren, nieces, nephews and other Charlie intimates assembled on the creek bank and stared at the bridge, beyond which sat Charlie's house and his pickup truck. Charlie sat behind the wheel, revving the engine impatiently.

Dewey stepped proudly out onto his handiwork and made a short, self-serving speech in which he painted himself as being virtually a peer with the men who designed and built the Golden Gate Bridge. With a flourish and the wave of his hand, Dewey signaled Charlie to move out.

Charlie shifted into first gear and moved slowly toward the bridge. He gingerly pulled onto the span and chugged forward. At mid-stream, he stopped and did a grandstand wave to the crowd. Bad move. With a loud SNAP! the span pulled loose and dropped Charlie and his truck into the middle of Hurricane Creek. Luckily for Charlie, the freshet was long gone, and the truck sank only to the bottom of the door windows. He managed to push the door open and to clamber onto the roof, where he remained in a sodden and sulky state until somebody found a fishing boat and rescued him.

Where was Dewey? In the excitement, he disappeared. I learned later from Annie that he hid out in her trailer until he thought it was safe to go abroad again.

"Well," I asked her with more than a note of triumph in my voice, "what did Dewey say caused his wonderful concoction to collapse?"

"Sorry rascal blamed me. Said I got him so distracted he mis-measured things. He was a'lookin' at his drawin's when I got back to the trailer that evenin'. Just studied things real careful, then turned to me and said, 'Damn that decimal point!' Seems he got an extra zero in there someplace, and that threw off his measurements a tad. Ain't seen him since."

This was hardly the end of Dewey's involvement with Great-Uncle Charlie's bridge. He took the Chevy place's wrecker out to tow the drowned truck out of the creek, got the wrecker stuck and got no help when he contacted the only other wrecker—at the Ford place—which was denied him because it eliminated for a time the competition.

Several weekends later, I chanced upon Annie. She was flirting with several pulpwood truck drivers, but she managed to spare me a few minutes because it was prior to payday, and the drivers seemed short on cash. I immediately asked for the latest on the Dewey disaster.

"He ain't here no more," she replied with more than a teaspoon of resentment. "I hear he has done run off with that lady preacher. Turns out he went to her tent meetin' and got right fascinated with her."

I had no problem with that.

"Does this mean we will hear Dewey's shrill voice on the radio, preaching along with Sister Sophie?"

"Naw! I heard her announce she was quittin' her radio preachin'. Now that she's free of false modesty, she's takin' her new self down to New Orleans. Says she's gonna start the Gospel of Good Things Curbside and Drive-Thru Ministry on Bourbon Street. Dewey is gonna play the drums in her band!"

Well! A rhythmic Elmer Gantry! No doubt that beautiful pair would attract more than their share of attention among the bizarre crowds jammed into that narrow, badly paved and incredibly noisy thoroughfare. Also, Dewey was now in a position to do no damage, except maybe to split a drum head when gripped in a moment of religious ecstasy. I mused on this for such a long time that I did not notice Annie responding to a driver whose dollars had suddenly reached the magic number of two. I thereby lost out on another chance of probing for Annie's last name.

Chapter 12

About Television and Taxes

It was a calm autumn afternoon when I pulled into Zenobia and, seeking the advantage of proximity, I headed on down U.S. 1 until a familiar string of honky-tonks and cheapie tourist motels began appearing. Figuring it was most unlikely that I would encounter Pulpwood Annie this early in the day at Bubba's, I turned into his undulating dirt parking lot and bounced into a slot close to the door. I was home for the weekend from the University of Georgia, and I was thirsty for what I could not find in my hometown—beer!

For all of Bubba's shortcomings—dirty floors, leaky roof, tasteless decorations, intellectually challenged clientele, bathrooms whose Third World-like befoulments defied clinical description—it was certainly on the cutting edge of technology when it came to electronic gadgetry. As soon as the local Rural Electrification Authority had strung wires out the highway, Bubba's had gotten hooked up. Immediately following was a succession of brightly lit and noisy jukeboxes, squawky radios and, eventually, a television set. South Georgia's first generation of TV broadcasts came from such distant metropolises as Jacksonville, Florida, Savannah and Albany, Georgia, with the only halfway dependable signal arriving through the ether and pine needles from the last-mentioned location.

Now, Albany is not exactly the cultural navel of the world. In fact, it isn't even pronounced the way most non-Georgians do it. To locals and others of southern Georgia it was Awl-BINNY, and when Awl-BINNY got a television license and began broadcasting, its signal was marginally clearer; thus, its fare soon constituted much of what those in its service area watched.

And since many of these people still remembered riding to town each Saturday morning in mule-drawn wagons, they were among the last to be able to afford those first large, heavy, black-and-white sets. This meant they spent inordinate hours standing in front of furniture or hardware stores that kept TVs running in their display windows to attract potential customers, or they went to places like Bubba's to see what was being broadcast.

Not that the fare was all that interesting. The three major networks, along with the fast-fading DuMont network, manfully provided evening feeds, leaving the local stations to stuff their morning and afternoon hours with crop reports, fashion shows, old cowboy movies, painfully crude kiddie shows and an occasional flannel-mouthed preacher. The really creative stations also cobbled together various kinds of talent shows as well. At the time, "south Georgia entertainment talent" was a virtual contradiction in terms, for there was precious little to be found and even less that stayed around once the gift became apparent. This meant the locally produced "talent" programs quickly became bogged down with nasal gospel quartets, lanky guitar players with bad haircuts and comedians with jokes fresh from *The Grand Ole Opry*, *Parts Pups* and *Captain Billy's Whiz Bangs*.

Perhaps the most interesting of these "talent" programs came from Awl-BINNY, the most notable and recurring sight on this television travesty being the master of ceremonies. The prime requisite for this task in tastelessness seemed to be greasy hair, an ill-fitting suit, an ear-to-ear grin that oozed saccharine sincerity and a completely tin ear when it came to recognizing talent. Such was Friendly Freddie, who tortured the airwaves each Saturday afternoon with his freak show of tone-deaf, ham-handed musical miscreants and lopsided tap dancers.

The Friendly Freddie Talent Scout Show was blasting away over the bar as I entered Bubba's domain, and glued to a barstool in front of the set was none other than the indelicate, indecent and indecorous

Pulpwood Annie.

She was completely engaged in watching a sluttish Lolita strum a guitar with more energy than melody while chirping, "A White Sport Coat and a Pink Carnation."

Annie, a creature on the wrong side of thirty, had entered her profession early, providing entertainment and release for the many truck drivers who hauled pine logs to the coastal pulpwood mills, thus acquiring her working name. Later, she expanded her craft to include denizens from Zenobia's dives and fleshpots. For some reason, she had taken a fascination to me, not that I ever partook of her questionable charms.

"Ain't she good?" Annie said without taking her eyes off the program as I threw a leg over the adjacent barstool.

"Yes," I replied somewhat archly, "and she must be a male in drag, a secret cross-dresser the likes of which wiregrass Georgia has not seen of late on the television. Wake up, Annie! That song's supposed to be sung by a man!"

Considering Annie's extensive sexual experience, it may be that women in white sports coats and sporting pink carnations in the lapels were a commonplace sight for her. Maybe they appeared in droves and were truly all dressed up for some sicko dance. At any rate, the subtlety of the scene had obviously escaped her, and it took a minute for Annie to tune reality in over the seemingly transsexual wails emanating from the tube.

"Oh," she said.

"How can you watch this abortion?" I asked as I silently signaled Bubba Sweat for a Miller. "*The Friendly Freddie Talent Scout Show* is undoubtedly the worst thing ever broadcast. If they start giving awards for really ghastly programming, Friendly Freddie will corner the market in trophies."

"Aw-w, it ain't so bad," Annie replied somewhat defensively. "It shore beats watchin' the walls of my beat-up ol' house trailer."

"Look who's getting hoity-toity about what she looks at," I responded. "Considering your line of work, you've spent more time staring at cracked ceilings and bug-filled light fixtures that any other ten women in the county! I should think your trailer walls would provide so many subtle designs in ketchupy fingerprints and purple paint smears as to keep you entranced endlessly. Friendly Freddie is a come-down from your own free show at home."

However, my spiel was falling on deaf ears. Friendly Freddie had a convert, and all my sarcasm would not create a crease one molecule thick in Annie's encrusted value system.

"Well, you can la-de-dah him all you want, but Friendly Freddie's givin' all them folks a chance to do their talent," Annie said somewhat heatedly. "Providin' their big break! Some Hollywood talent scout may be sittin' in a place like this and see that ol' girl and decide on the spot to offer her a contrack!"

Pulpwood Annie had seen too many movies. The next thing would be for me to light two cigarettes in my mouth and hand one to her, a la *Now, Voyager*!

The conversation might have led to mortal combat, but Bubba sauntered up about this time, glanced at his pocket watch and announced to nobody in particular that his wrestling match was coming on, and he was switching to a Savannah channel. Goodbye Friendly Freddie and the dustbin of regional talent.

"So," I said in my most expansive tone, "what's been going on since last I sought to avoid you, dear Annie?"

"I been dodgin' the tax collector, that's what!" Annie fired back. "Ever since Squirrel Johnson got elected to that office, he's been tryin' to get me and the other workin' girls to pay taxes on our earnin's."

Annie paused to discover she was deficient in suds. She yelled for Bubba, who reluctantly tore himself away from the TV just as Gorgeous George was attempting to remove the foot and lower leg of Man Mountain Landis. Bubba ran a draft, handed it to her and pointed to me as warning that I was now responsible for her tab. Bubba quickly returned to the program, where he and a gaggle of Jeeter Lester clones were raptly observing a silver-haired octogenarian clobber the referee with a folding chair. I began to think Friendly Freddie might be a better alternative, after all.

A loud sucking noise in the vicinity of Annie's lips and the frosty glass preceded her continuing commentary. Even I was impressed as the liquid level dropped precipitously. If she weren't so shopworn, she might have been a good party girl for the boys in my frat.

"Squirrel claims I owe back taxes!" Annie continued. "Back taxes! I earn my livin' on my back, and he wants to tax me for it! Told him over and over he can't tax me for earnin' money doin' an illegal ack! Sorry rascal don't see it that way and says he's gonna report me to the sheriff if I don't pay up soon!"

I knew something about Squirrel Johnson. The possessor of two beaver-like front teeth, Squirrel played passable baseball as a kid, but during his early teenage years a less-than-nimble batter swung his Louisville Slugger a bit low and caught Squirrel squarely on the back of his curly blond head as he crouched behind the plate. Alas, Squirrel's days as catcher were over, and so was his plan to join the Army and make a career of driving a tank around Fort Riley, Kansas.

In his rattled state of mind, Squirrel was fit for little except elective office, and since the dogcatcher liked his job, it fell to Squirrel to run for the next most unpopular political opening, the county tax collector. It figured that somebody with Squirrel's marbles-loose-in-a-gourd intellect would zero in on a person like Annie and try to shake her down as a tax dodger.

There was little I could do about Annie's tax problem, and so I let the matter drop. After quaffing a few more brews and shelling out hard-earned cash for Annie's prodigious thirst, I departed. It was several months before I had the chance to return to Zenobia, and when I did, I naturally ran into Pulpwood Annie at her favorite low-life hangout. She was in rare form, flirting and laughing with a group of boeotians who gathered around her near one of Bubba's battered pool tables. Her knotted hair tossed and shook as she cavorted amongst the guileless gropers, her squinty eyes sparkling with what they no doubt mistook for tantalizing fire. Of course, she broke off from this choice collection of white trash as soon as she saw me pop through the door.

Not being one who is bashful about reminding another human

being of bad news, I immediately inquired as to her status with the money-grubbing tax collector. I figured it might scare her immediately into earning some dollar bills from the raffish friends she had so recently abandoned, thereby leaving me in peace. When will I ever learn that when it comes to shaking Annie, I am eternally star-crossed?

"Oh, phooey," Annie replied with a disdainful shrug that almost dislodged her tacky, imitation-leopard Frederick's of Hollywood mini-dress. "I ain't worried about that! Fack is, I ain't ever gonna have to put up with any of Squirrel Johnson's crazy ideas."

Well, that was news and most heartening news at that. A person no longer in fear of the tax collector! Maybe it was catching. Maybe she had learned a secret I could use when I started earning money from sources other than bumming off long-suffering family and friends or mowing neighbors' lawns.

"I don't believe a word of it," I responded laconically, hoping to stir Annie's feisty competitiveness and to secure insights into her evasions with the tax man. Of course, my tactic worked to perfection.

"It's true!" she informed me in decibels loud enough to crack tooth enamel. "He ain't never comin' back around me no more! We fixed him good!"

Was this the editorial "we," or did Annie recruit allies? I pushed on.

"What do you mean, 'we'?"

Annie looked like she was ripe to burst with information, but she instinctively evaluated her environment, determined a mighty thirst was descending and resolved the matter by demanding that Bubba supply her with a beer. I ordered another and dolorously signaled I would pay for both.

"It was me and my cousins what did it," Annie said as she slurped down her drink. "Maybe you know them. There was Tizzie, Megan and Alec."

I knew about them. Tizzie and Megan were offspring of Annie's notorious Great-Uncle Charlie, with the mother strongly suspected as being one of Charlie's many bastard daughters. Both women plied their trade along traditional family lines, whoring up and down the tourist highways of south Georgia. Tizzie was barely five feet tall, and aside from her quite easy virtue, her only other discernable talent was the capacity to convert everything she ate into rolls of fat that collected on her stocky body like quivering cables of Jell-O.

Megan tended toward height, standing a full six feet tall, assisted in part by her decidedly pointy head. Had she tried out for the Wicked Witch in *The Wizard of Oz* movie, she would have won the role hands down. Without makeup.

As for Alec, he was one of the few legitimate products of Great-Uncle Charlie's well-used loins. Not that he was that much to brag about. Alec was, as they say, a little light on his feet, often donning the clothes of a female relative and hanging around the Zenobia bus station, trolling for "fwiends."

If this was the gang that helped Pulpwood Annie rid herself of the dreaded tax collector, then God help Squirrel Johnson! I could not imagine what the unholy confederation had concocted.

"Well," I managed to say while digesting this rather uncomfortable lump of information, "you must fill me in."

Annie did so with a relish. Seems that Squirrel kept pestering her until Annie could stand it no more. She sought out her cousins and asked for their advice. Turned out Squirrel had been badgering each of them, also, and especially Cousin Alec, whom Squirrel repeatedly referred to as a "prevert." Alec took offense, claiming he was a woman trapped in a man's body and ought not be taxed for it.

The solution to their problem involved some old-timey backwoods methodology that still was recognized if not particularly honored in the county. From time immemorial, and especially during the poverty-stricken decades following the Civil War, debts were often paid in kind when coins were not available. Thus, doctors received hams and chickens for delivering tenant farmer babies. Lawyers collected bags of collards and turnips for drawing up wills. Storekeepers ran tabs on groceries and sent out monthly reminders in the forlorn hope that their customers would have some harvest-time cash to pay down on the bills. Thus, products from the land and services from its homely and often destitute people enabled many to meet their debts, or at least to make an occasional dent in them.

This was the card the cousins played on Squirrel Johnson. All contacted Squirrel, with the three women promising hitherto unknown physical delights and unspeakably erotic connections. Alec said he would wash Squirrel's truck. Squirrel sent word back that he would be by soon to collect.

Annie chuckled devilishly as she remembered what happened next.

"We tole him to come out one particular night to this ol' tenant house way out in the county," she said. "We knew it was abandoned, but Squirrel didn't. Well, he pulled up in his ol' truck just after dark. Us girls was waitin' on the porch and led him inside. Tole him we was gonna be in three rooms, and he was to take his pick for who he went to first, second and third. 'Course, he chose me right off 'cause I'm the best lookin', if you get my drift."

Thought of those aesthetic alternatives sent a shiver through my spine.

Annie apparently lured the gullible Squirrel into what passed in the gloom for a bedroom and urged him to undress. This he did with dispatch, flinging his clothes in a corner. Erect and randy, Squirrel was so engrossed in embracing Annie that he did not hear footsteps in the hallway and became aware of another presence only when the door flew open with a bang. A male form framed the doorway, a shotgun in his hands.

The apparition demanded loudly who dared to deflower his innocent daughters and followed by discharging a round of buckshot into the ceiling. An eardrum-shattering blast echoed through the empty house followed immediately by the sound of shattering glass, for the naked Squirrel had dived through the nearest window. In the process of escaping, he inflicted upon himself numerous contusions and stinging cuts upon his head, torso and protruding manhood. Fortunately, Squirrel's early athletic skills came to the fore, enabling him to regain his feet and sprint with great dispatch into the nearest cornfield.

Whap! Whap! Whap! came the sound in diminishing explosions as Squirrel plowed through the alien corn. Soon the noise of his headlong plunge amongst the stalks faded, when, unexpectedly, a coon hunter in a nearby swamp opened up on a critter his dogs had just treed. The gunfire apparently caused Squirrel to think he was being besieged from another angle. Suddenly, the sound of smashed cornstalks began to grow louder as the terrified tax collector dashed back toward the house. A series of increasingly loud Whaps! announced Squirrel's arrival on the road.

Naked and cut, bleeding and bruised, terrified and confused, Squirrel dashed mindlessly to his truck, and since he had left his key in the ignition, he was able to turn the crank, shift into gear and roar away. However, Cousin Alec had done more than pose as an irate, shotgun-armed father. He had found a yellow jacket nest and had carefully lodged it under the blanket Squirrel sat on in the truck. Squirrel's frantic entry masked the feel and sound as he plopped down on the yellow jacket nest, and it was only after he had traveled a short distance down the dirt road that the stunned insects rallied to wreak vengeance for their crushed homeland.

"Lordy! You shoulda seen that truck, zigzaggin' down the road with yeller jackets a'streamin' in and out the window," Annie said. "We laughed till we fell down and rolled in the dirt, it was so funny! We heard later that when he finally got to the emergency room at the Zenobia hospital, the doctors pulled three dozen stingers out of ol' Squirrel—and three of them from his pecker! And guess what else! We ain't heard a peep outta that tax collector since!"

As usual, Annie's story left me speechless. I drained my glass and pondered ordering another round. Annie anticipated me and placed the order instead.

"So, what now? You are free of the tax man. What else does life hold for you?" I asked somewhat hesitatingly.

"I'll tell you what I'm gonna do next," she replied firmly. "Me and the cousins is gonna get in my truck next Saturday and drive over to Awl-BINNY and enter Alec in *The Friendly Freddie Talent Scout Show.* Gonna have him sing "A White Sport Coat and a Pink

Carnation." He can't help but win 'cause he'll be wearing my brand-new imitation-leopard dress from Frederick's of Hollywood!"

A grand mal headache struck me like a thunderclap. An incredible Pulpwood Annie story had again done its work on my defenseless brain. That was enough. I dismissed myself, paid the tab and departed, making mental note to be sure I was deep into north Georgia during the coming weekend, far from the malignant airwaves surging from a certain television station in Albany, Georgia. Of course, in my haste to leave, I forgot again to inquire as to Pulpwood Annie's last name.

Chapter 13

As to the Sticky Fingers of Darlene Faye Stone

Dirty laundry piled up to my eyeballs, a car with the gas gauge seemingly locked permanently on "empty," and with zero aspects for securing a weekend date with one of those round-heeled university coeds everybody else was supposed to be enjoying ad infinitum, I decided to bum a ride home. The prospects of clean clothes, decent meals and the hope of hitting my family for a few precious dollars overrode whatever mixed feelings I had about returning to the gritty little south Georgia town from which I was spawned.

Arriving home that Friday evening at a fairly early hour, I decided that after expressing my greetings at warp speed to the mandatory parents and relatives, I would gather up Mother's egg money and invest it in some Millers over in Zenobia. Borrowing my grandfather's car—while he wasn't looking, of course—I sped down the highway and barely made it to the Zenobia American Legion before my Saharan thirst completely shut down my windpipe. This noble establishment, for which a highway marker of some kind ought to be erected, was known from coast to coast for selling Canadian Club and Seven-up for only twenty-five cents a glass.

I can prove this. Once, while enrolled in a graduate course at the University of Hawaii, I met a fellow about my own age. We told where we were from, and when I identified my hometown, he asked, "Isn't that near Zenobia?" Surprised, I nodded in the affirmative. "Well," he continued, "I was flying from Ohio down to Florida a few years back, and our private plane developed some trouble. We landed at the

Zenobia airport, and while the repairs were underway, we took refuge in the American Legion." He paused, and his eyes got a bit misty as he added, "It's the only place in the world where I have been able to buy all the Canadian Club and Seven-Up drinks I wanted for two bits each."

But I digress.

The long and the short of it is that I spent all of Friday evening and a chunk of early Saturday morning tossing quarters at the Legion's genial bartender. Came the morn, and I and my grandfather's car chugged slowly back into his driveway. If red skies at morning are the sailor's warning, you should have seen the look on my grandfather's face when he got up earlier than usual, went for his copy of the *Atlanta Constitution* and discovered a curious vacancy where his dependable old DeSoto had previously been parked. I quickly fabricated a story that I was passing by, saw one of the tires was low on air and hot-wired it so I could get it to the filling station for repairs. To prove my good will, if not to mask my tendency toward absurd prevarication, I volunteered to eat breakfast with him. Figuring my grandfather would be too shocked to respond—I usually avoided him like the plague, and he knew it—I was myself rattled when he said, "Sure, come on in."

It was not rosy-fingered dawn that held a vise-like grip on my forehead as I staggered into the house. I was working on a world-class hangover, and the swollen tendrils of the remnants of my brain reminded me with fulsome authority that it was going to be a long day. I slouched into the breakfast room and slumped into the nearest chair.

"Say grace."

Sluggish silence.

"Say grace!"

This time it penetrated. Grandfather wanted me to bless the very food that I was about to get nauseated over just by looking at it! I couldn't escape! Closing my eyes—that was the easy part—I mumbled forth rapidly, "Lord-bless-this-food-to-the-nourishment-of-our-bodies-and-Sigma-Epsilon-Chi-to-Thy-service-Amen." Only when I managed to pry one eye open and saw the astonished look on Grandfather's face did I realize I had inadvertently chanted the mantra used endlessly at my fraternity house. Oh, well, I figured Grandfather was catholic enough in his view of what the Almighty wanted and for whom the Almighty did what he did. As it was, Grandfather rolled his eyes toward the chandelier, muttered something akin to glossalalia but which sounded suspiciously like "stupid sonovabitch" and turned to his scrambled eggs and ham.

A few bites of food, six hours of sleep during the heat of the day and an ice-cold shower, and I was ready for a reprise in the sinkholes of Zenobia. I knew the DeSoto was going to be off limits for the next millennium, give or take a century or two, so I turned my boyish charm on Mother and conned the family car keys from her. Came the dusk, and I was surging southward toward some suds.

Having singed my cranium the previous night at the American Legion, I wisely decided to try some less potent brews at Bubba's. This was not an obvious option, for by entering Bubba's scruffy abode, I ran a better-than-even chance of encountering south Georgia's premier seller of tail and teller of tales—the redoubtable Pulpwood Annie. However, the clientele and fistic tendencies at Kelley's, the Green Grotto and other even more dubious enterprises along U.S. 1 pretty well narrowed my choice. And my fate.

Sure enough, the Princess of Prostitution sat astride a barstool, wearing her tackiest miniskirt, providing an ample display of undesirable leg and busily engaged in charming and offering at bargain-basement rates her somewhat overused body to a burly farmer-type. Annie was the one who bragged that when she got started in the hooker business, she commanded ten dollars a trick, which usually was one "missionary" with no extra charge for the wash-up. The contemporary market being what it is, and with Annie no longer able to offer her all in its pristine entirety, she still could get ten dollars for her effort, but it came in two-dollar increments.

The gods were smiling at me. No doubt, Fatty Arbuckle would come up with a couple of George Washingtons and would figuratively and literally occupy Annie for enough time for me to down a few drafts. Who knows? Maybe he would go for the record and keep her out all night!

I was midway through my first glass when a volcanic eruption of choice Anglo-Saxon vulgarities, sharp questions about one's legitimacy and strong hints as to one's genealogy being directly connected to Old Dog Trey filled the fetid air. I looked up. Annie and her rotund rube were nose to nose, calling each other such salty slanders that I wished later I had taken notes. The boys at the frat house would have loved them.

Oliver Hardy made some final remark about Annie's fee being three dollars too high for a two-dollar whore and stomped out. Annie gracefully hurled a Blue Ribbon longneck, neatly whacked him on the back of his fat, layered neck and proffered the sincere wish that he would catch his balls in a barbed wire fence.

Honor, if not order, restored, Annie sashayed over to where I was and, sans invitation, planted herself on the adjacent barstool.

"Stupid!" she said to nobody in particular.

"Who, me? Or your late pal, Porky Pig? Or are you shooting for all the population endowed with testosterone?" I drawled.

"Lucky!"

"Well, Annie, I won't try to interpret that unless that's how you see me, being as I get to share company with you this evening. Limited to glittering conversation only, as usual."

Ignoring the hint that I was not a viable paying customer, Annie reached for my glass and began sipping from it. I made a mental note to sip from the far side of the rim that had been marked by her Carnival Red lipstick. Then, flash! I remembered a story by Isak Dinesen about a woman who contracted syphilis from kissing the toe of a religious statue that had just been wetly smacked by an infected man. Life can imitate art all it wants, but I was not going to risk mine by sucking up one of Annie's spare spirochetes when I could order a new and reasonably clean glass from Bubba. Annie did not or chose not to notice.

"So, who's stupid and who's smart?" I recklessly pushed.

"Darlene Faye Stone, that's who," Annie blurted.

"And who's that?" I asked. "Some soiled dove you met during a marathon whore-in at an all-night truck stop? A bimbo from Ludowici who rolls drunks for a living? One of your high-toned relatives who knits socks down at the factory?"

The Empress of Insensitivity scratched a somewhat hairy armpit, took another sip from what had been my glass and then rendered the judgment, "Your beer tastes funny." Pushing it aside, she ordered a fresh draft and with a nod told Bubba to add it to my tab. Lucky me. Now she was developing sign language to complement her motor mouth.

"Of course, Darlene Faye has always been kind of stupid and lucky at the same time," Annie observed to nobody in particular. "I guess I ought not to 'uv been surprised."

"Considering that interesting combination of karmas probably applied to just about every south Georgia female who has turned a trick with the horny flotsam and jetsam of the region, I hardly see why her behavior should stand out in your mind," I said. I was baiting her, hoping to provoke her into seeking out some trade among the great unwashed that were bellied up to Bubba's bar instead of wasting my time with this wacky story.

No luck, as usual. Annie ignored my barb and launched into her story as though she had been succored by the poet laureate of the United States.

"Well, you know that her boyfriend breaks into banks. Runs with those Dixie Mafia types the FBI is always talking about. He makes these trips and comes back to see her days later with a pocket full of frog eyes."

"What? Frog eyes? Why would he be out gigging for frogs? And why keep their eyes, for God's sake? I thought all you ate were the legs!"

"No, Mr. Know-It-All. Frog eyes is what you get when you burn into a bank safe. The torch drops little bits of melted safe into the money, and it burns little holes in the bills. They call 'em frog eyes 'cause that's what they look like, and that's what Elmore Tittle specialized in. Frog eyes. Gave a handful to Darlene Faye every time he got back. Said it was to discourage her from shopliftin'."

"Whoa!" I said. "I thought this story was going to be about a bank burglar. How did shoplifting get into it?"

"Shut up and listen." Annie replied. "That's the trouble with you fellers with edjakashun out your bunghole. You axe too many questions, and you inerrup' people who know what they was tryin' to say."

Properly chagrined if not stunned by this unexpected censure, I clamped my lips together and tuned my ears in Annie's direction.

"So, Elmore come back from this job, see? And he saw all this dime store stuff Darlene Faye had lifted, and he gave her a good ass-kickin' to get her attention. Tole her over and over to never steal anything small. 'Steal somethin' that will be admired,' that was Elmore's policy. Also, he kept at her to keep her hand in the whorin' game 'cause it would produce as much as a hundred a day when she worked the conventions in Savannah or Macon."

"There's nothing like unselfish support from one's family and friends," I interjected while almost choking on the combination of Hav-A-Tampas and other cheap tobacco products that were key elements fighting for space with the oxygen in the barroom. Naturally, the shifting clouds of nicotine and airborne coprolitic particles were mother's milk to Annie, and she seemed more inspired with each lung-rotting gulp of atmosphere that she drew into her bruised and badly decorated body.

She continued, "Anyways, Darlene Faye and Elmore was visitin' some of Elmore's bank robber cousins over at Dothan. Elmore had this real pretty watch he had got during a heist, but he didn't like the band on it. So, Elmore took it to a Dothan jeweler to have another band put on it. Darlene Faye went with him, and while Elmore and the jeweler was goin' over the watchbands, she saw there was no one else in the store, so she reached behind the display counter and stole a handful of diamond rings. Said later they had price tags from ninety-nine dollars to two hundred ninety-nine dollars—cheap for diamond rings but a right smart amount when they was all added up."

"Wait a minute," I interjected. "You mean this Darlene character shoplifted a bunch of diamond rings, and nobody saw it?"

"God's truth," Annie replied. "'Course, when she and Elmore got back to the house, she showed what she got, and Elmore got really pissed off. Started yellin' at her that now he couldn't go back for his watch 'cause the jeweler would rightly figure the missin' rings went missin' while he was lookin' at the watchbands. Smacked Darlene Faye up side her head a few times and was generally workin' his way to givin' her a world-class ass kickin', if you get my drift."

Getting Annie's drift was about as difficult as falling out of bed. She provided "drifts" in her stories so often that if her "drifts" took on a geographical form, she would have "drifted" the length and breadth of the Gulf Stream just on the stuff she had told me.

"Yes, yes, get on with this story," I yelled. "I am beginning to get a headache trying to figure out what other numbskulled stuff your stupid friend pulled." And I reached for a comforting Miller.

"Well," Annie huffed, "as I was saying, big-time trouble was brewin' for Darlene Faye, and all Elmore's relatives was busy listenin' in. Just as Elmore was gettin' ready to walk Darlene Faye down to the woods where he would deliver a few Sunday punches, his Uncle Hiram stepped up, told Elmore to cool it for a few minutes, then left."

Annie paused for dramatic effect. I couldn't wait for what was coming even though one-thousand-watt flashes of cerebral discomfort had started pinging inside my head. I was beginning to feel like a U-boat undergoing depth charges from the entire United States Navy.

"You see," Pulpwood Annie whispered in a conspiratorial undertone much akin to the roar of a twenty-horsepower Snapper lawn mower, "Elmore's uncle had killed at least three men with his bare hands, and what he said usually got done, or there was consequences. So, Elmore sat on his anger, just a-simmerin' and a-waitin' for the chance to really lower the boom on Darlene Faye. 'You dumb broad,' he kept mutterin'. 'Stupid as a stick!'"

"And so? Does the uncle come back with a chain saw with which to chop up the unsuspecting Darlene Faye? Is she branded on the forehead with an 'S' to designate a congenital shoplifter?" I was running out of logical alternatives for this latest Pulpwood Annie story.

"No, no," she replied patiently. "Pretty soon the uncle comes walkin' in the door and tosses somethin' over to Elmore. Guess what? It was Elmore's watch from the jewelry store! The uncle also had a bagful of some other stuff. Do you get what happened?"

Confessing a complete lack of imagination for what the uncle's murderous/criminal inclination of mind was, I arched my eyebrows to signal "What now?" and awaited the denoument.

"Don't you see?" Annie said exasperatedly. "Uncle Hiram was a pure Southern gentleman. Rather than allowin' little ol' dumb Darlene Faye to get beat up worse than a pizza crust, he took hisself down to that jewelry store and robbed it! And stole back Elmore's watch! Plus a whole bunch of other stuff! Everything worked out just swell! Elmore got his watch with the new watchband, he let slide givin' Darlene Faye an ass-whippin', and she got to keep all them diamond rings she stole! And the uncle hauled in enough swag that after he sold it to a fence, he had enough to take the entire family to Daytona Beach for a week!"

Well, why not? Did I really expect her to concoct a story that defied illogic? Where else could I have had my intellect jerked and tugged, if not expanded, in such bizarre company? And from whom else but Pulpwood Annie, south Georgia's storyteller par excellence, who never got around to telling me her last name.

Chapter 14

Annie and the Dixie Mafia

"Did I ever tell you about the time I run with the Dixie Mafia?"

Pulpwood Annie was perched, as usual, on one of the rickety, tall stools that fronted the bar area at Bubba's. Given a few drinks and a forgiving nature, one would think they looked like a raggedy, red, Naugahyde-and-wood surf line. Annie inhaled a world-class draw of smoke from her Lucky Strike, blew it deliberately in my face and coyly studied to see whether her news or the carcinogenic blast would confound me the more.

She got the answer in spades. I reeled from both.

"What?" I blurted out, coughing and blinking from the twin assaults upon my previously undisturbed person. "I know you've performed every heterosexual act in the Kama Sutra, but I didn't have a clue that you were a crook as well!"

Annie waxed indignant. "I ain't no crook and never have been! I just got with a bunch of them once, that's all!"

Her dignity and what she perceived as her unsullied reputation restored to full satisfaction, Annie turned to Bubba and ordered another round of Millers for us.

"Put it on his tab," she blithely murmured.

Ever a sucker for one of Annie's unpredictable stories, I nodded agreement to Bubba, figuring the cost of a few beers was small pay for what I was sure would be an account far beyond either my experience or imagination.

"Okay," I said, "I know a little about that bunch. They are a gaggle of Southern good ole boys who burglarize stores and banks and steal cars all over the old Confederacy. So, how did you get involved with them?"

Annie was now in her element. She had my undivided attention, a free beer in hand and a favorite recollection about which she could yak indefinitely. Also, it was early afternoon on a hot Friday in August, and her regular customers were still at work, driving pulpwood trucks, plowing fields or knitting socks at the local factory. What better way to fill the time before she started earning her two-bucks-a-pop living than regaling a smart-aleck college boy with her rag-tag-and-bobtail experiences?

"It was before your time," she said breezily. "I guess it started with Rudy Rouse. Or was it Donnie Dean? Maybe Julius Caesar Mincey and Pussycat Boatright? I can't rightly remember. Anyhow, they was all mixed up in it."

The alliterative pair of Rudy Rouse and Donnie Dean I knew about. Both were local hoi polloi who had inhabited the county jail on numerous occasions after being involved in such "epic" criminal events as Saturday night brawls, petty shoplifting, peeing in the street and similar social offenses one would expect from such residuum. But Julius Caesar Mincey and Pussycat Boatright? What manner of men were these? Not that it would have mattered much to Annie's bargain-basement standards.

"I guess it all started when I was workin' out of them Ludowici juke joints. Takin' on them Yankee tourists comin' off U.S. 17 and them soldier boys from Fort Stewart.

"There was this illegal dice game goin' on almost always in one of the back rooms at The Shady Tree Truck Stop, and I started droppin' in to see what the action was. Sometimes even got a customer before he lost it all in the game," she said.

"You've lost me on the first turn," I interrupted. "What does your penny-ante hooking have to do with the Dixie Mafia?"

Annie glared at me.

"I have tole you, and I have tole you! Stop bustin' in with your smart-ass questions about what I'm tellin' before I've had time to tell you! Now, hush up or bug out!"

Oh, was I sorely tempted to take Annie up on her offer! However, the lure of a juicy, beyond-Beyond story kept me from grabbing my beer and buzzing out the door.

"Okay, okay! I'll go stand in the corner, teacher!" I replied.

Thoroughly enjoying the moral high ground, Annie gave me a smile that would have turned rancid butter sweet. She ran her nicotine-stained fingers down the side of her latest Frederick's of Hollywood T-shirt, which mysteriously proclaimed in large letters that she was "Missed Opportunity 1942," and rummaged successfully in the pocket of her pedal pushers for a well-used tube of bright red Maybelline lipstick. She applied it liberally in the general vicinity of her lips, blotted the effort with a napkin and deigned to enlighten me further.

"That's where I first met him," Annie recalled brightly. "The great Pussycat Boatright! You shudda seen what that man could do with a pair of dice! Had a special way of bouncin' them bones off the back rail of the table. I seen him walk the numbers from two to twelve without missing, and that was with a pair of fair dice! He told me later it all had to do with the surface of the table and the back rail."

"Well, Mr. Pussycat Boatright obviously did not need you to distract his suckers while he burned them with loaded dice," I dared to comment. "But I still don't see the connection."

"Maybe I oughtta stop and tell you that joke about the cow and the jackass walkin' to town. The jackass keeps askin' how much further, and the cow keeps sayin', 'Patience, jackass, patience.' Over and over, the same comment and same answer, and finally the person listenin' gets tired and wants to know when the joke will end. The one tellin' the joke then says, 'Patience, jackass, patience.' Same goes to you!"

And so Annie proceeded with her tale. As was so often the case, I had to rearrange and summarize what she said in order to understand the flow of events. This was because Annie specialized in asides, just-thought-ofs, maybes and what-ifs galore. The bare facts seemed to be this: in his prime, Pussycat Boatright possessed two qualities that made all the difference to a person like Pulpwood Annie. First, he was catnip for the ladies, possessing slick black hair, a trim mustache, Van Dyke beard and flashing dark eyes. A smooth operator whose Cherokee bloodlines came through clearly, he maneuvered silkily through crowds like a sly snake. His second "virtue" was that he was somewhat dangerous, for he circulated among the criminals and lowlifes of south Georgia, shooting craps, playing cards and—eventually—becoming a part of the Dixie Mafia.

"What was his real name?" I foolishly asked.

"Don't matter. Pussycat was what ever'body called him, and it fit him tighter'n a pair of cheap shoes. Guess his name was a natural, bein' as 'it' pretty well described his favorite interest next to shootin' craps," she replied. "He didn't hanker for cats, neither, if you get my drift!"

After asking around Bubba's later that evening, I learned that Pussycat was the direct descendant of that pride of Zenobia—Wildcat Boatright—who was renowned throughout the region for his willingness to scrap with anybody over any issue at the drop of a hat. One fellow said the carving on Wildcat's tombstone read, "I'll Fight You From a Wheelchair if Necessary." It was obvious that Wildcat's son chose a less violent and more physically rewarding method of taking on an "opponent": by screwing or rolling dice. Both seemed to pay off continually for him.

It was also obvious that Annie was as drawn to Julius Caesar Mincey as she was to Pussycat. He was another farm-grown reprobate, who made an early decision to live the good life by taking from those who had more than he did. After serving four years with the U.S. Marines, Julius tried his hand at running a drive-in restaurant in a town near Zenobia. Unfortunately, he spent more time in his new Chevrolet convertible schmoozing the town's sweeties than he did selling burgers and fries. He was bankrupt within a year, and this moved him directly into more illegal lines of work.

The way Annie described Julius, he was one of those golden lads, standing more than six feet tall, tanned and fit with curly blond hair. His chiseled good looks, bright blue eyes and chalk-white teeth combined with an easy smile to make him a favorite among both men and women. Like his namesake, Julius Caesar Mincey radiated leadership. For additional effect, he liked to go around with his shirt unbuttoned almost to his navel in order to show off his hairy chest and bulging pecs. In the words of Annie, "He was a hunk!"

"Julius got him a tattoo on his arm that was the Marine emblem," Annie also recalled admiringly. "Showed an anchor and a rope and the motto—'Simply Vitalis' or somethin' like that."

Having been scolded twice about my commentary, I chose not to enlighten her that the Marines greatly treasured loyalty—fidelis—far above a brand of hair tonic.

"Funny thing is, Julius and Pussycat both claimed there never was a Dixie Mafia," Annie added almost as an afterthought. "Said it was somethin' the FBI invented to make them look swell when they pinched some Southern boy for a crime."

"Nevertheless, the term stuck," I added. "I recall reading all sorts of newspaper stories about such-and-such a burglary, robbery or car-theft ring involving the Dixie Mafia."

"One thing for sure. They wasn't mixed in with them crooks up North. Julius and Pussycat tole me they never hung tight like them Italian Mafias do. They'd get a few guys together for one job and an entirely new group for another. Jes' depended on who was available, who was in the pokey and who was in the hospital recovering from a whuppin' or a knifin'."

"How democratic," I said with a yawn. Annie's description of the order of battle for a Dixie Mafia job was putting me to sleep.

"Yeah, that's how come Julius and Pussycat got Rudy Rouse and Donnie Dean involved. They would need somebody to do the heavy liftin' or somethin' a stupid guy could handle, so they'd whistle for Rudy or Donnie. Julius and Pussycat was always the brains behind their jobs."

"You mean you were not a consultant for their crime wave? I'm shocked, shocked," I inserted in my best Claude Rains imitation.

Annie obviously had not seen *Casablanca*, for she continued to rattle on as though my words were in purest Swahili—unintelligible and irrelevant.

A new thought obviously flashed through Annie's brain. "Oh, lemme tell you about the way Julius and Rudy got to know each other," she said excitedly. "Early in his career, Julius got caught one night breakin' into the Oldsmobile place. Just that afternoon, he had paid cash for a new Rocket 88, and he was tryin' to get into the building to steal back the money before it got deposited in the bank the next mornin'."

It was a fascinating tale. The judge sentenced Julius to three months in the county public works camp, where he was assigned to what was called a bully squad. This choice group of misfits, drunks and petty crooks worked on the dirt roads and the swampy sloughs. Much of the work involved trying to shovel out ditches in water-filled depressions, a most inefficient method but quite satisfying if the major goals were back-breaking labor and virtually no soil removed from the area.

Julius sought escape from this by smart-talking a guard. Thus, he ended up in "the hole," a tiny punishment cell well away from the PWC's main dormitory. Guards took all his clothes and gave him a single, dirty blanket to wrap around himself. A piece of bread constituted his daily meal, although every third day he was issued a serving of the convicts' regular supper.

One particular meal featured fried chicken, and Julius kept the well-picked bones to suck on during the next few days. He did not pay attention when a nearby "hole" cell gained a new occupant. Growing increasingly hungry, Julius decided to eat the chicken bones and began carefully chewing away. The crunching sound carried to the neighboring cell.

"Whatcha eatin'?" a voice asked.

"Chicken bones," Julius answered.

"Well, please don't chomp 'em so loud," the voice responded pitifully. "You're shore makin' me hungry!"

Of course, the fellow desperado was Rudy Rouse. The two struck up a friendship that continued after both were paroled and as Julius began cutting his swath across the South with his many criminal activities.

Whereas Julius was larger than life and charismatic, Rudy was a quiet, stringy little runt. He had thinning brown hair. His dark brown eyes constantly darted up and down, right and left, as though he were continually checking to see if someone were skulking about, if a bird happened to be flapping overhead or if his fly were unzipped. It was fortunate that Rudy was strong and could carry the tools of his criminal trade, for he was incapable of reading words of more than one syllable or of planning anything more complicated than a peanut butter and jelly sandwich.

However, Rudy's diminutive stature sometimes came in handy in those early criminal days. He and Julius began burglarizing small-town banks across Georgia and Florida. This involved stealing an acetylene torch and tank from a car repair shop, hauling the bulky, heavy load to the bank, breaking into the bank at night and cutting a hole in the bank's safe. Rudy's small hand and arm could then be thrust into the hole to extract whatever cash was within easy reach.

"I never went on any of Julius's or Pussycat's jobs," Annie was quick to inform me. "I sorta moved between the two of them as girlfriend of the moment. They seemed to kinda enjoy the swappin' around. That meant I was back at the motel or apartment when they would come back with the night's haul."

One of her favorite Julius-and-Pussycat capers involved their effort to break into a loan company office located in a Brunswick strip mall. They chose a Sunday night to hit the office, figuring nobody would be in the building. They cut a hole in the roof, dropped down into the darkened store and discovered to their dismay they had landed in the ladies' dress shop instead of the loan office next door.

"Talk about mad! Them two fellers was fit to be tied! There was only a few hours until dawn, and they didn't have enough time to break into the roof over the loan office," Annie said with a laugh.

"So, what did they do?" I asked. "Leave a note of apology?"

"Naw! They rounded up all the evenin' dresses and other nice stuff, bundled 'em together and hoisted 'em up through that hole in the ceiling. They give some of them dresses to me to sell to my workin' girl friends and took the rest over to Savannah and put my friend Indian Lil to work sellin' the rest. Made a right tidy sum for a night's work in the wrong place!"

"I can see I have chosen the wrong profession," I snidely observed. "I should have become a professional dress stealer in order to rise high amongst my peers within the Dixie Mafia."

Annie smarted from my stinging rejoinder. "Now you jes' hold on a minute! They was in plenty more jobs that got them a whole lot more! Listen up!"

Apparently, becoming a Dixie Mafia regular required a period of apprenticeship and/or on-the-job training. Neither Julius nor Pussycat brought any discernible knowledge of the craft when they launched their criminal careers, and they had their fair share of screw-ups and near-disaster experiences before they become proficient and professional. Annie said one of their learning experiences involved trying to steal a safe from a Savannah grocery store.

The two men had spotted the store and had noticed that the building space next to it was unfinished. Plywood sheets spanned the front window areas, concealing whatever might take place behind them. Again striking on a Sunday evening when all stores in the little shopping complex were closed, they drove their car—a beat-up Pontiac Bonneville—into the alley and broke through the rear door of the unfinished store. They then proceeded to knock a large hole in the wall separating the unfinished store from the grocery, planning to roll the safe through the hole and over to the car.

The plan began to unwind at this point. The safe was far heavier and bulkier than they had anticipated. Struggling manfully, they used boards and pipes from the unfinished store as levers to fudge the safe, inch by painful inch, toward the car. Two stout planks served as an incline up which the safe was pushed and tugged to get it into the car's trunk. However, when the heavy safe dropped into the trunk, the weight lifted the front end of the Pontiac. This disengaged it from being locked in "park," and the car began rolling slowly down the alley. The frantic burglars chased after the vehicle and managed to get it under control just before it coasted into the street.

"The weight of them two men in the front seat gave the front wheels enough traction that they could drive it with that heavy load in the back. I never saw such wore-out men in my life!" she said with a cackle. "They was so beat by the time they got back to the motel, they didn't have the strength to pry that safe open, much less go a round with me! They threw a tarp over the trunk and collapsed on the bed. After a good night's sleep, we drove out to the woods, and the boys used their crowbars to pop the safe open. They got about eight thousand dollars from it!"

"And two hernias at no extra charge," I opined.

Annie ignored my unsolicited comment, perhaps because she was so familiar with the anatomical areas in question that she knew neither man had experienced a rupture from his encounter with the errant and elephant-like safe.

She continued: "You gotta keep in mind that back then, when them boys was runnin' wild and rackin' up two or three safes a night, it was before stores and banks began installin' all them safety alarms they got nowadays. They did most of their work at night, didn't have to hold up nobody, and took enough dough for them to live in a mighty fine style."

I found it hard to believe some of the things her Dixie Mafia lovers did. In one instance, Pussycat and Donnie Dean went looking for something to burgle in a backwater hamlet situated along the Georgia coast. Donnie, another glowing product of the south Georgia educational system, spotted a sign over a certain building.

"Hey, Pussycat, what does b-a-n-k spell?" he asked.

"Bank. Why?"

"Just wanted to know. Think I saw one back yonder."

Approaching the target at night, they prepared to break open the back door. However, Donnie spotted something suspicious about an adjacent window. Shining his flashlight on the sill, he saw to his amazement that the window was slightly ajar. All they had to do was push the window up and crawl into the bank.

Once inside, they saw the vault door was going to be too difficult for their primitive equipment. The disappointed duo almost left empty-handed, when Pussycat realized that the wall flanking the vault door was brick.

Trusting his instinct, he swung a heavy mallet against the wall. Several more swings, and the mallet went through the wall! In no time, the men had expanded the hole large enough that they could crawl inside, where they thoroughly rifled stacks of cash and safe deposit boxes.

"Pussycat give me a big ol' bracelet he got from one of them safety boxes," Annie boasted. "Kept it for years before havin' to pawn it to help pay for repairs on my truck."

At this point, Annie's thirst triumphed over her desire to fill my ear with more Dixie Mafia drivel. She turned her empty glass upside down and yelled for Bubba to get her a refill. Being as I was the one paying for her drink, I decided I had better get a fresh brew in case my foamy lukewarm glass had become a fly's swimming pool while I was not looking.

Refreshed through the miraculous effect of a Miller gushing down her throat, Annie resumed command of the situation.

"'Course, the main thing I liked about the Dixie Mafia fellers, aside from the money they spent on me when they was flush, was the way they looked after each other," she said. "One of them get in a fix, the others would pitch in to help. When Donnie got caught tryin' to steal a milk truck up in Chattanooga, they all made up a pot of money and offered it to the governor to buy Donnie a quick parole. Almost worked, 'cept the governor got indicted for somethin' else and had to resign!"

Then, there was the time when Rudy ended up in the pokey for stealing several thousand dollars' worth of stamps from a Vicksburg, Mississippi, post office. He had planned to sell them wholesale to a gang that specialized in pushing stolen cigarettes and other small but desirable items. The transaction was to take place in a small riverfront cafe, but a deputy sheriff taking a doughnut break overheard the men talking and arrested them on the spot.

Rudy was housed on the second floor of the county jail. He

immediately sent word to Julius to come get him out. Julius rounded up Pussycat, Donnie, Annie and a couple of others and drove all night from Zenobia to the Mississippi town.

They discovered the jail backed up to the Mississippi River, and the best way to get to the rear area where Rudy's cell was located was to approach the building at night from the river.

"So, we got busy and stole us a boat," Annie said. "The boys also stole a cuttin' torch and tank to pass up to Rudy so's he could get through the bars. The night they was to break him out, they cranked up the motorboat and headed upstream to the jail."

Although Annie remained, as usual, at the motel where the group was staying, she apparently knew all about what was to happen and, even more interestingly, what actually did occur.

Arriving unseen in the dark, the men docked the boat, hauled the equipment across the sloping lot behind the jail, flashed a cigarette lighter to alert Rudy and waited for him to respond. Sure enough, a light flickered in one of the barred, second-story windows.

The first unanticipated problem popped up when the rescuers realized the jail's second story was actually three floors up from where they stood, for a basement not visible from the front had been built into the sloping riverside. This meant they had to get a ladder.

"Julius was always thinkin' ahead, and he recalled seein' this volunteer fire department buildin' down the street from the jail," Annie said. "So, he sent Donnie and another guy to go steal a ladder from there. They was back in a flash with a ladder just tall enough to reach the window where Rudy was."

The second unanticipated problem developed when Julius started up the ladder with the cutting torch. As he passed the first-story window, he heard several female voices. He peeked into the window and saw three teenaged girls staring at him. They were juveniles being held for some petty violation. Noise from the ladder's being put against the wall alerted them to what was occurring outside, and they began rapping on the window to get Julius's attention.

"Hey, what you doin'?" one of the girls asked.

"Hush!" the startled Julius hissed angrily at them.

"Hey, we're hungry!" another girl said insistently.

All became clear. Jailhouse blackmail! The girls would scream for the guards unless the rescuers got them something to eat. Julius scrambled down the ladder and told Donnie to haul ass to the nearest cafe and buy a bunch of burgers and fries.

Several precious minutes passed with agonizing slowness before a sweaty Donnie came stumbling back with his arms full of bulging, greasy paper sacks. Julius started up the ladder again, this time pausing at the girls' window and distributing the bags of food to them.

"Now, keep your damn mouths shut, or I'll come back and cut your tits off!" he growled.

The girls were too busy eating their burgers to pay any attention to his obviously empty threat.

Julius began another trip up the ladder with the heavy, awkward-to-handle cutting torch and fuel tank. He thought the rest was going to be easy. Not so.

The third problem came when Julius reached Rudy's window. Seems Rudy was sharing a common holding cell with the town's prime collection of drunks, deadbeats and drifters. All wanted to depart with Rudy!

Julius had no choice.

"Cut your way out and make damn sure you crawl out the window first," he ordered Rudy. "We'll leave the ladder for those stumblebums to use if they can figure out how to come down without wakin' up half the damn town!"

"What happened next?" I asked when Annie suddenly decided to clam up and to survey the crowd for a paying customer. After discerning that I remained her best alternative, she returned for what Paul Harvey calls "The Rest of the Story!"

Rudy apparently was better at cutting jailhouse bars than he had been at selling purloined government stamps. He was out and down the ladder almost before Julius reached the ground. The men ran quickly down the slope to the boat, cranked it up and chugged out to midstream. In short order, they had traveled downstream to the point where they had hidden their getaway car. They abandoned the boat, piled in the car, drove back to the motel and picked up Annie.

"Talk about a crowded experience! Goin' back to Georgia with all them men in the car! They was sweaty and dirty from all that rescue work, and that damned Rudy hadn't bathed since he had been put in the calaboose! I like to have stifled myself to death!" Annie indignantly informed me.

"I am so glad you survived," I responded. "Otherwise, the world would never have known of such Olympian heroics. No doubt, Julius, Pussycat and their fellows-in-trade will someday get medals from the Kiwanis Club or some similar group."

"They didn't want no medals!" Annie said with a huff. "They just wanted ol' Rudy out so's he could help them hit some more banks!"

"Okay, I'll buy that, but I have a question: what did those fellows use all that stolen money for?"

"Mainly on girls like me! Livin' high! Buyin' big, fancy cars and speedboats! Drinkin' and partyin'! You see, they figgered there was always more dough to be taken when they needed it. Didn't none of them open savings accounts, far as I know. Although...."

I sensed another chapter in Annie's Dixie Mafia saga.

"Although what?"

"Well, there was that time when Julius and Pussycat thought they would open a nightclub over in Waycross. They spotted this empty building out U.S. 1 south of town where all them motels was springin' up. Thought it could be a goldmine. Thought they might go legit."

It was some idea of legitimacy! After pushing Annie for all the sordid details, I learned that this "nightclub" was intended to supply not only drinks but also the services of Annie and her female associates. It was to be nothing more than a glamorized cat house!

Using some of their pilfered cash, the two men leased the building—a low-slung wooden frame affair with a sizable asphalt-paved parking lot—and then spent several weeks "investigating" similar dives in Jacksonville and Savannah for decorating ideas and for an appropriate name for their business. Once they sobered up from their marathon drinking/whoring spree, they came up with the "original" idea of painting the interior black. Free neon signs from the local beer distributor would provide most of the interior lighting, and a juke box would illuminate the tiny dance floor adjacent to the bar. Added atmosphere would be burlap-wrapped posts with plastic palm fronds attached to suggest a South Seas ambiance. A huge, blinking neon sign over the doorway would proclaim the establishment's name—"South of Your Border."

Considering that a fair amount of the expected revenue would come from body projections and orifices south of the anatomical border—so to speak—it seemed the name was quite appropriate.

I was enamored of this perverted step toward free enterprise.

"Tell me more about the nightclub. Tell me that it was a success. Tell me that it became franchised nationwide!" I insisted.

"Well, it did get off to a good start," Annie countered. "Couldn't help but make money, bein' as how the booze they was sellin' didn't cost them nothin'."

Further enlightenment! Free liquor! If I learned the secret of this achievement, I could parlay it into getting elected president of my fraternity!

"Liquor that did not cost them anything! Tell me how they managed that!"

Annie's account at this point became so garbled with meandering afterthoughts that I had trouble deciphering her recollection, but the gist was this: Pussycat had spotted an isolated liquor store near Walterboro, South Carolina. Housed in a small, concrete block structure and separated from other buildings by overgrown vacant lots, it fairly begged to be rifled. This Pussycat and Julius did one dark night, using their trusty sledgehammer to knock holes in the rear wall with a few mighty swings. They filled a rented U-Haul truck with case after case of scotch, bourbon, gin, tequila, champagne, various liqueurs and mixes. Loaded to the gills, they drove west along U.S. 17, over the Talmadge Bridge at Savannah and thence to their Waycross nightclub.

All that remained, they thought, was to scrape off all those South Carolina tax stamps that were glued to the bottles. "After all, they didn't want no health inspector to look behind the bar and find a bunch of South Carolina bottles!" Annie pointed out.

"That makes sense," I said. "But what did they put the liquor in, if they didn't use the South Carolina bottles?"

"Glad you asked. Dawned on them fellers they couldn't use unstamped bottles no more than they could sport South Carolina tax-stamp bottles. So, they rounded up me and the girls who was gonna work the joint and sent us to Brunswick and Savannah. We had to go through the dumpsters and trash cans behind all the night clubs and clip joints there and bring back empties with Georgia tax stamps on them. Talk about a smelly job!"

"I suppose you ladies succeeded in your worthy but odorous task?"

"Well, we shore found out that Georgia folks drink some strange brands of booze. Had one hell of a time findin' empties of the more popular brands."

"How come?"

"'Cause the bartenders take cheap booze and pour it into the fancy bottles, that's why! Next time you're in a bar, look at the bottles on the shelves. Bet you see plenty with worn labels! You can bet the farm that bartender's servin' you Ol' Radiator 'sted of Ol' Granddad!"

"Then, I gather your employees enjoyed a bounty from bar sales, if not from what you peddled on your back."

"Not for long. Seems the FBI had been watchin' Julius and Pussycat and made a pretty strong case against them for burglarizin' a bunch of banks. They had to sell 'South of Your Border' to pay their lawyers' fees. Put me out on the street again, but they went to prison."

"And you continued with the other Dixie Mafia types?" I asked.

"Naw. The cops and feds was gettin' pretty good at bustin' them. Most of the fellers I knew ended up serving time."

"Speaking of which, quitting time is at hand, and your customers will soon be queuing up for a go at you. I had better split, but before I go, I want to know what eventually happened to your pals."

Annie noticed the front door opening to allow several scruffy truck-driver types in. She sensed an opportunity, but before leaving, she provided the answer.

"I'll tell you next week. I'm goin' over to Reidsville to see Julius and Pussycat durin' their next visitin' period. They got adjoinin' cells at the White Elephant! Understand they come up for parole in a year or so!"

I suppose it was good to know that the Georgia State Prison had a nickname, and it came as no surprise that Annie was fully aware of this. It also came as no surprise to me as I drove north toward home that I had again missed the opportunity of pushing Annie for her last name.

Chapter 15

Annie and the Scar Crapps Saga

It really blew my mind that Annie had been ensnarled at one time with certain Dixie Mafia types, and I was glad for her sake that Pussycat Boatright and Julius Caesar Mincey were serving time in Reidsville. As "harmless" as bank burglars and jailbreak artists might be in the pantheon of criminal activity, they still were men who easily circumvented society's standards in pursuit of a quick buck. Who knows what they would do if cornered or somehow got Annie involved as an accomplice?

I was praising her one evening over our usual round of Millers as to her perspicuous decision to distance herself as quickly as possible from those lowlifes.

"Yes," I opined with all the wisdom of one who has just shed his nineteenth birthday, "you might have ended up in a passel of trouble by continuing to run with that bunch."

"Who says I didn't?" Annie replied with more than a touch of ire in her voice. "Who says I never trucked with any other criminals? They was lyin' through their teeth if that's what's bein' said about me!"

Whoa! What was she revealing? Was I astraddle a Naugahyde barstool only inches away from somebody's moll? What had the loose-lipped Annie failed to tell me? Bubba's joint seemed to be morphing into a hangout for gun-totin' guys and their tough-as-a-razorstrop gals.

"Okay, I possess no psychic powers, even if I made a C in

Psychology 101 last quarter," I confessed. "Tell me about your travels with John Dillinger, Babyface Nelson and Pretty Boy Floyd. Or was it Bonnie and Clyde?"

"Never heard of them fellers. What pulpwood outfit do they drive for?" Annie said in a tone of boredom that strongly inferred I should stop haranguing her in order that she could launch one of her *Iliad*-like stories.

So, I shut up.

But Annie just sat there, slurping her paid-for-by-me beer.

"Come, now! Surely your brain is not so pickled with booze that you've forgotten your 'Ten Most Wanted' pals," I said.

"Naw, I was jes' recallin', that's all."

"I can't wait to hear what you have recalled."

Of course, I didn't have to wait. Out poured a typical Annian tale. This time, it was about the repellant Scar Crapps.

Another fine, fresh-from-the-farm felon, Scar Crapps grew up on a one-mule plot located ten dusty miles from Zenobia's greater metropolitan area. His Christian name disappeared long ago, for he acquired his nickname after having his right cheek permanently incised when as a small child he fell against a red-hot wood stove on which his slatternly mother was stirring a mess of 'possum and greens.

Automobiles were certainly commonplace when Scar was growing up, and many a country family piled into a pickup or a rattletrap Model T for a bumpy ride to town on Saturday. However, the Crapps family was of that last-of-a-thousand-generations group who was dependent upon animal power for transportation. Thus, they hitched their mule to a wagon and clip-clopped into Zenobia every Saturday, tying up to an oak tree located near the depot.

Country-come-to-town had real meaning in those days, for bad roads and long distances kept these rural peasants from leaving their farms any more often. And even if they could, they usually didn't have enough change in their pockets to justify a trip to town.

Saturday in Zenobia was the antithesis of Zenobia from Monday through Friday, when business was so slow that merchants closed down at noon each Wednesday. The big marketing day was Saturday, and hordes of farmers, their wives and daughters often arrayed in flour-sack dresses, their sons sporting slicked-down, Brilliantine-coated hair and/or army uniforms, drifted around the courthouse, walked into and out of stores, sipped moonshine from Mason jars, swung by the jail to hear a leather-lunged Holiness preacher whooping it up for Jesus, argued politics, tossed pennies, got into alley fights and then shopped for their store-bought necessities in the final, frantic minutes before Zenobia's merchants wearily closed their doors at 10 p.m. sharp.

The whittle-and-spit crowd congregated along a wooden bench adjacent to the local drug store and spent the afternoon and evening swapping lies about crops and women. And not necessarily in that order of importance.

The country folk also went to the Saturday movies, even though Zenobia's Roxy Theater would never have been confused with the similarly named, elaborate film palace in New York. Instead, it was a narrow, dank building with folding wooden seats that clacked and banged whenever somebody raised or lowered them. A balcony with even more battered seats housed the coloreds who, in those days of legislated segregation, had to sit virtually in the rafters in order to get their dime's worth of entertainment. The smell of stale popcorn added an appropriate atmosphere to this cultural icon.

It was at the Roxy that Scar's true character was formed. Like most kids of his age, he arrived in Zenobia with ten cents in his pocket to use as he saw fit. That meant buying a ticket at the one and only movie house, where he could see a color cartoon, a cowboy shoot-'em-up, a Republic serial, a B-feature and assorted previews of coming attractions. Some moviegoers get their kicks from enjoying the fantasies on the big screen. Kids like Scar saw selected acts as guides for future behavior—especially if the acts involved mayhem, violence and cruelty.

This I found out one evening while slumming in the low-life Green Grotto. I happened to mention Scar Crapps's name to one of his boyhood contemporaries. The fellow roared with laughter as he told me about the time he and Scar went to a cowboy movie in which the Indians buried a white prisoner up to his neck, then ran their horses over his exposed head.

"Hell, Scar said he could do that!" the man recalled. "Got him a shovel and a couple of dominekker chickens from his momma's flock, buried them birds up to their necks and run over them with a dadgummed lawn mower! Boy! Was his momma fit to be tied when she learned about that!"

I added that the Crapps's resident rooster was probably a bit miffed about having to experience a decrease in his love life, also, but this salty observation sailed right over my companion's head.

Other information from Annie filled in the gaps in Scar's metamorphosis from mean kid to meaner adolescent. Scar's male hormones apparently kicked in earlier than for most boys his age, for he was soon squiring and having sexual encounters with girls and women several years older than himself. On one occasion, he and a twenty-year-old slut were enjoying an evening at a local dive when three men tried to make moves on the woman. Scar whipped out a pistol and shot all three—none fatally—and ended up serving time in a Georgia reformatory. He was fifteen.

Having "graduated" from this school for criminal enhancement, Scar was ready to begin doing and being what he had seen and admired on the silver screen when he was an impressionable youth. Illegal slot machines, poker and dice games were endemic in the American Legion posts, VFW clubs, Moose halls, juke joints and truck stops throughout coastal Georgia, and Scar was soon a regular feature in them. He usually had a girl with him, and that's how Annie entered the picture.

"First ran into Scar over at the VFW in Jesup," Annie told me. "He was real handsome, and he was right polite and courteous when he was sober."

"A temperate Rhett Butler, I presume."

"Yeah, as a matter of fack, he did seem sorta like that feller in the movie—tall, thin, dark hair, mustache, and he had a real commanding voice. And, somehow, that slash on his face made him real appealin' to us girls!" Annie almost blushed as she added, "Them was my glory days. Looked like a million bucks and earned plenty from Scar and his crowd!"

I struggled silently and unsuccessfully to imagine the vision Annie must have presented when at her best.

According to Annie, Scar played to win when he gambled. He apparently was a "mechanic" with cards—capable of dealing himself and others whatever high or low cards that would enable him to win the pot. I also learned he had another way of making money from these games.

He told her about an arrangement he had with some pals who would burst into a particularly high-stakes game just as the pot was flush with money. Wearing masks, the men would wave pistols and shotguns at everyone in the room and would then proceed to rob them all—cash, watches, rings, anything of value. Scar would be "robbed" also, but he would get back his valuables and a sizable cut of the swag when he met later with his pals to divvy the loot.

"'Course, once in a while it sorta backfired," Annie said. "I remember him comin' back to the motel where he was to meet the guys who had robbed a game where he was playin' earlier in the evenin'. Turned out one of the robbers wanted to make it look good so he bullied Scar and kicked him in the backside before takin' Scar's wallet. Problem was, just before the robbers broke up the game, Scar saw one of the players—a big fat man—stuff a wad of cash into one of his shoes.

"Scar chewed the overly eager robber out. 'Well, I just was tryin' to make it look real,' the man replied. 'Yeah, and if you hadn't been so busy kickin' me in the ass, you'd seen me signalin' you to search that fat man's shoes for the thousand bucks he had stuffed there!' Scar replied."

"Every line of work has its built-in perils and problems," I cleverly countered. "No doubt, Scar and his minions used that one as a learning experience."

"Yeah. Scar told me he wasn't never gonna use that SOB again on a job!"

As was the case with most of Annie's regulars, there were

individual episodes that she remembered with relish and projected toward my quivering eardrums with all the delicacy of a tidal bore rushing upstream.

As had been proved in his adolescence, Scar was quick to carry a weapon and, apparently, just as quick to use it. He took Annie to Savannah one weekend, telling her he and a pal planned to break into a department store that Sunday night, after everybody had gone home. Sure enough, the two men climbed to the roof and quickly cut a hole over the store. It was night, and there were no lights on inside the building.

"Ol' Scar was first one down the rope into that store," Annie recalled. "Soon as he hit the floor, he turned and almost had a heart attack! There was this big man standin' right beside him! Scar pulled out a pistol and let him have it. Blam! Blam! Blam!"

"Oh, my Lord, Annie, you were an accomplice to a murder!" I exclaimed.

"Not hardly! Scar just shot the stuffing outta a store dummy in a man's suit! Couldn't tell it was a fake in all that dark! Spooked Scar and the other man so that they shimmied back up that rope and got the hell away from that building before somebody reported gunshots!"

"I suppose the next thing you are going to tell me is that dear Scar never harmed a fly after that. Learned his lesson and became a member of the Salvation Army, carrying a loaded Bible instead of a rod."

Annie yawned at the predictability of my reaction and interpretation of events. She checked her glass of beer, reasoned her account of Scar merited another round and made sure that Bubba got the message. Sure enough, two foamy glasses appeared along with a less-than-gentle reminder from Bubba that he did not allow callow youths to run large tabs at his bar.

I went to Hip National and planked down the necessary dough.

"I shore liked travelin' with that man," Annie observed to no one in particular, although she was clearly projecting her volume over a jukebox that was vibrating under the impact of an extra-high-decibel rendition of Phil Harris's "That's What I Like About the South!"

"So, where else did you go, and what mischief did you two get into?" I asked.

"Mainly, we went to all them gamblin' places where Scar liked to play. He almost always walked away with winnin's, and that made it real nice when it came time to order dinner! 'Course, he always was a gentleman and paid me for my time and stuff. Long as he was sober, that is. Oh, and we also went to them rooster fights up in South Carolina."

Justifiably known as the Gamecock State, South Carolina boasted numerous illegal pits in its rural counties. Sporting men from all walks of life would traverse miles of lumpy dirt roads in order to stand shoulder to shoulder around a small, walled area. They shouted out wagers and covered them with cash. Two roosters with sharp metal spurs attached to their feet were baited, then were thrown toward each other. The winner walked away. The loser was fit only to be somebody's Sunday dinner.

"Did Scar and his buddies ever try to rob a cock fight?" I inquired.

"Are you crazy? 'Course not! All them bettin' men came with money to gamble and guns for protection. Scar said if he ever tried to hold up that bunch, he'd be shot full of holes before he could get out the words, 'Hands up!'"

"I'm sure that's good to know in case the irresistible impulse seizes me to stick up a South Carolina cock fight," I replied.

"Pigs will fly before you do that, sonny boy," Annie came back with more than a touch of sarcasm.

"Then I trust that our paragon of Southern gentility always kept you safe from harm and the sheriff?"

"Naw, and that's why I broke up with him, too!"

"Really? What was this cause celebre?"

As usual, Annie had me plying her with questions. She would do just about anything to prolong this delicious moment, and if she couldn't think of anything else to do, she would call time out to readjust her underwear.

She hopped off the stool, stretched, groped at her waist to make sure her fishnet-style pantyhose were situated comfortably in an area I never cared to visit, plumped her somewhat sagging bosom and then deigned to rejoin me for her concluding report.

"Yeah, I decided it was better to keep on livin' instead of runnin' with that wild man. See, we was over in Waycross one Saturday at some club, maybe a VFW, and Scar had been drinkin' pretty heavy. Drinkin' always made him mean, and when we walked into this joint, Scar got into an argument with a man sittin' at the bar. I had gone to the ladies' room and didn't hear how the scrap got started, but it had somethin' to do with which man had the biggest, well, you know what.

"They kept yammerin' back and forth. Suddenly, Scar whips out his pistol and starts firin'! The other guy has a gun, and he begins shootin' at Scar! Point blank! You wouldn't believe the noise—gunshots, shouts, screamin' women!

"I ducked behind a table and stayed there 'til it got real quiet. Looked up, and there was Scar, sorta wobbly, holdin' his bloody side and standin' over this man lyin' face down on the floor.

"'That'll teach you to say your dick is bigger than mine!' Scar said."

"What happened after that?"

"Me and Scar got outta that place before the police showed up. Learned later the man was dead with half a dozen slugs in him. Scar just got nipped in the side. I bandaged it up for him right good. But I didn't want no more part of shootin's, and so first chance, I got myself back to Zenobia."

"Sounds like Scar was a prime candidate for a room at the White Elephant over in Reidsville. Maybe a roommate with Pussycat or Julius. I assume he was eventually caught and jailed."

Annie laughed at the thought.

"Naw, Scar never served no time. A couple of weeks after the killin', this guy who claimed Scar owed him money went to Scar's place. Demanded the dough, and when Scar didn't cough it up, that feller pulled out a big ol' pistol and shot Scar Crapps fulla holes!"

"How awful!" I said with as much fake sympathy I could muster after having had one Miller too many.

"He had a right nice funeral," Annie responded. "Looked real good!"

I reserved comment on that old Southern habit of complimenting a corpse on his or her lifelike demeanor.

"So, what now?" I ventured to ask.

Annie looked at the clock on the wall and eyeballed the crowd. I figured she had determined that it was unlikely she would find a paying customer that night.

"I think I'll turn in. Got a chore to do."

"What in the world do you have to do that would interfere with your turning a trick tonight? Surely, there's somebody here with two bucks to spare."

"Don't matter none. Talkin' about ol' Scar brought back memories. Got me to thinkin'. He left me his pistol, and I ain't oiled that sucker in a while. Don't want it to get rusty."

With that, Annie unplugged herself from the barstool, aimed for the door and was out and gone before I had the wit to realize what a sentimentalist she was. I also had again failed to consider the matter of her mysterious last name—the one I could never seem to discover.

Chapter 16

Into the Philosophic Mind of Pulpwood Annie

Pulpwood Annie and I were in a deep discourse over the different value systems expressed by most males and females. Somewhat surprisingly, she was rather expansive in her view of both.

"Us girls are like great big ol' radio stations. The Good Lord made us—or at least some of us—to broadcast our stuff whether we intend to or not," she admitted, preening at the thought. "Fellers can't help it any more than a boar hog can when a sow's in heat. 'Cept us girls are a bit more regular than a sow usually is."

Having had more than my fair share of truly lamentable blind dates, I said I sometimes saw more parallels between sows and women than she was allowing for.

"'Course, I make my livin' based on the idea that men want women a whole lot more than women want men," Annie said. "Shore would be a strange world if women went around propositionin' men, pinchin' their butts, promisin' all sorts of trash just to get into their pants." She paused and then added it might be a real good learning experience if men had to endure this kind of fascination from the frailer sex.

I quickly confirmed that I prayed daily for such a role reversal. "I am ready to be abused," I promised.

"No, you ain't," Annie said with more than a spoonful of venom. "You turn down every chance I offer to get you between the sheets. Ain't I loaded with what all them college girls have who give it away for free?"

"Yes, Annie," I replied. "You have all of that and more. Especially what the epidemiologists would love to explore at length under microscopes. I really do not have a desire to have my name applied to some exotic new disease contracted from you. And in all likelihood, posthumously."

Annie's titanium-coated self-esteem ricocheted my invective out into the atmosphere. She was unwaveringly undaunted by my round-the-clock rejections of her preposterous connubial offers.

She returned to the conversation with suspicious agility.

"Truth is, college boy, the basic problem between men and women is plain ol' mathematics."

That stunned me. Being really lousy in all forms of mathematics, algebra and geometry that extended beyond counting my digits, I wondered, first of all, how a ninny like Annie could come up with such a concept and, second, where she would get the vocabulary to defend it. We were seated at a booth in the rear of Bubba's, and in order to buy time while I pondered this weighty tome, I signaled to a waitress.

"Ruby Pearl, bring us two Millers," I said with the authority of a man who had two five-dollar bills tucked into his wallet to accompany a somewhat badly folded and, I suspect, fatally compromised "secret weapon" that I had been unsuccessfully carrying around for months. Maybe Annie's insights would give me a chance to use it before it turned into rubberized dust.

Ruby Pearl, a derelict who dropped into Bubba's to take on Annie's leftover customers, had become a double-dipper, working the crowd for waitress tips in between ventures to a nearby vehicle where she consummated her more financially rewarding job. There was little about her to admire. She had stringy brown hair, thin lips, Deputy Dawg cheeks and a figure that seemed to have been inspired by a pine sapling. However, there was enough essential female attached to her frame to provide her with an occasional pass from a myopic male.

As long as she kept her fingers out of the top of the longneck beer bottles she brought to our table, I felt it was relatively safe to drink from them. She took the order, shuffled toward the bar, warded off lunges by a chubby pool-playing yahoo and returned with the order.

"Okay, give me the bottom line. How does math figure into the man-woman equation?"

Annie gave me a look to determine if I were paying attention or just placating her, as I often did when she began to ramble. Placating had evolved into my only defense for mental health if I were to continue listening to her far-off-the-chart stories and experiences, all of which she divulged at any opportunity. Convinced that I was alert and properly focused, she began.

"Well, it goes like this," she said. "Like I said a minute ago, men are all the time wantin' women, but most women ain't as hot for them. So, women have to make up all sorts of reasons to dodge the men—headaches, late to work, that sort of thing."

"Yes," I replied. "I have a ledger full of those rationalizations, all registered from personal experience. So what?"

"So, men get horny and start lookin' for other outlets, of which I am a prime example. Then, their women get mad and turn off the sex even more. Leads to all sorts of problems. I bet I've contributed to half the divorces in this neck of the wood, in one way or the other!"

"What a wonderful heritage," I commented. "You must enter that upon your resumé."

Annie took a pull on her longneck beer, ruminated a minute, then returned to the topic at hand.

"Now, the math problem enters in how men and women look at gettin' sex," she said. "'Course, I jump at every chance 'cause it's money in the bank, but I ain't got the typical female's attitude toward gettin' laid."

To which I nodded a quick affirmation.

She continued. "Suppose a man wants to get some first thing in the mornin', and the wife says, 'No, I ain't got time.' He comes home at lunch, and she can't come across because the baby's cryin'. That evenin' she's busy fixin' dinner, but finally, at bedtime, she says, 'Honey, let's do it,' and they do it."

My blank stare signaled I did not get her point. "Good for him," I said, somewhat puzzled. "Better late than never."

"Exactly my point," Annie said excitedly. "To the wife, he wanted it, and she provided it. To the husband, he had four opportunities and scored only once. There's the math: for her, she was a hundred percent sexual provider. To him, it was twenty-five percent! No wonder I get so much bizness!"

Well, I was dumbfounded at Annie's revelation. I had never thought of sex in that light. Maybe it was because I wasn't getting any on a regular basis, making those rare and infrequent liaisons as high points in an otherwise dull, celibate undergraduate existence instead of some kind of significant, anthropological advance.

I began entertaining thoughts of introducing Annie to the social studies faculty at the university. Maybe I would become a second Freud, Kinsey, Krafft-Ebing or Ellis. Then I had second thoughts: that bunch of ivory tower dreamers at the university was light years away from being prepared to take on Pulpwood Annie, even if it were limited to conversation. And knowing Annie, who's to say she would limit it to that?

When in doubt, I fall back upon the Socratic method. I posed a question.

"So, what is the answer? Sexual math for the momentarily deprived? Imagine the homework involved! I would volunteer to break ground for this course, even if I am a Mongolian idiot when it comes to numbers. In fact, this is one course I would not mind repeating," I said with a relish.

"Don't have no answer," Annie said. "I guess the differences are there for a reason that most folks just don't get. 'Course, I'd just as soon keep things as they are. When it comes to sex at home, my motto is 'Less is More.' The less sex there is, the more I can earn!"

And just as though it were planned, a lanky man dressed in a plaid shirt and jeans entered Bubba's, looked around, spotted Annie and headed directly to our booth. Ignoring me as though I were another empty beer bottle, he leered at Annie, winked and made as to sit down beside her. Annie frowned, stiffened and refused to budge.

"Now, don't high hat me, Pulpwood Annie!" he said loudly. "It's

Saturday night, I just got paid, and I want to get laid! Up and at 'em!"

"I ain't interested, LeRoy. I don't need your money, and I ain't goin'," she replied. "Go talk to Ruby Pearl. She ain't particular who bangs her in the back seat of her Buick!"

An animated conversation ensued, most of it unprintable but quite revealing as to the depth and breadth of knowledge each possessed about scatological samplings and how they might be projected into the other's various orifices. Or how much might be found between the other's ears. I was fascinated. Maybe this was data the school of public health ought to know about. I considered taking notes.

The debate climaxed on a less than lethal note, although there were several opportunities for this option as well. Annie established beyond reasonable doubt that even she had her limits, and the man rejoined that he would rather take on Ruby Pearl any day of the week even if Annie got down on her knees before him and, among other things, begged him to reconsider.

Mexican standoff completed, LeRoy stomped over to Ruby Pearl, who was eagerly waiting well within range to hear the whole, turbulent diatribe. She took LeRoy by the hand, flashed a triumphant smirk at Annie and headed out the door.

"Rubber popper!" Annie shouted at LeRoy as he departed the building.

H-m-m-m! That was a new invective.

"Okay, Annie," I said. "I give up. What's a rubber popper?"

She gave me a look as though I had just been let out in the yard for the first time. Then, apparently realizing the answer required certain limited, specialized knowledge, her look softened.

"Well, it ain't as though you're likely to experience it," Annie said. "What happened was this. LeRoy and I was doin' it one evenin', and after he had his fun he just kept a-layin' there, hopin' for a quick recovery. Fat chance for that little weenie! Anyhow, he finally rolled over, but his 'rubber overcoat' had slipped off. Stuck in me like a cockleburr!"

Her face clouded with anger at the recollection, then continued.

"I guess there ain't no eddykit for what followed, but when he reached to get back that rubber, he pulled at it, and it slipped out of his fingers and gave me a loud pop! Right on my goodie! Stung like blue blazes! LeRoy thought it was so funny that he popped me two or three times before I got that thing away from him! Since then, he's been nothing but a no-good rubber popper to me, and I ain't takin' any more bizness from him," she said with finality.

Well, I had learned something. There was a penalty to be paid if one treated Pulpwood Annie's goodie with a tad too much disrespect!

Annie got up, stretched and readjusted her Frederick's of Hollywood dress—the one that featured a plunging neckline and a slit-up-the-side skirt that sought almost successfully to meet somewhere dangerously near the middle.

"Gotta go," she said. "Just caught a signal from a customer."

I glanced down the room and saw the pudgy pool player who had manhandled Ruby Pearl beckoning not so subtly in Annie's direction.

"Okay," I said. "And thanks for the illuminating discourse on the male and female condition." I got up and started for the bar, since the lone waitress was undoubtedly spread-eagled in her Buick and working for something other than tips. A cool longneck would be perfect to top off the evening.

Annie and Minnesota Fats were conducting a fast negotiation that concluded as two dollars exchanged hands. As I walked past them, she said out of the corner of her mouth, "Ferget all that stuff I rattled on about, college boy." And, flashing the two paper bills over her head, she added, "Here's the only kind of mathematics that really counts, if you catch my drift!"

And away they went.

I guess she was right. Supply and demand were now congruent, and at least in this instance, both male and female were not only sure of what each wanted, but both were confident they would quickly collect on their desires.

I raised my beer bottle to Pulpwood Annie in salute, took a swig and promptly remembered I had forgotten again to ask her about her last name.

Chapter 17

Conclusion: Pulpwood Annie Reprised

Graduation from the University of Georgia came eventually for me, and I bade dear old Athens a sad farewell as I prepared to meet my draft board's decree that I dedicate the next two years to Uncle Sam. This I did in a drafty old World War II barracks, after which I spent the next couple of decades as a journalist and working at a variety of colleges and universities. My hapless home town and nearby, siren-like Zenobia became fading memories, for I seldom returned except for short visits with my fast-diminishing family, the older members of which were crossing the bar in rapidly increasing numbers.

It was the wedding of a cousin's child that lured me again home, and while I was in town, I thought I would run down to Zenobia and see if it was still the way I remembered it. And, who knows? I might find Pulpwood Annie still cranking out tricks.

Returning to an area after a lengthy absence is almost always a shock and a disappointment, and Thomas Wolfe was right on the money when he wrote that one could not go home again. Old landmarks along the road had disappeared or had become dilapidated. New houses, clearings and businesses sprang up unexpectedly. As for that stretch of U.S.1 south of Zenobia where all the alluring honky-tonks had once been located, none remained. Instead, franchised pizza parlors, hamburger stands and ice cream emporiums stood gleaming where the Green Grotto, Kelley's and Bubba's Bar once radiated tacky neon splendor.

Only the American Legion building remained, and it seemed a bit embarrassed at the company it was keeping, for hedges and bushes now grew up almost as tall as the one-story brick structure to mask what had once been one of my favorite watering holes. Oh, well, any port in a storm. I parked my car and went inside.

Mid-afternoon never was a prime time to frequent a place like this, and the only life forms I saw were a bartender and a few old farts sitting at the bar, discussing some obscure point relating to the Battle of the Bulge. From the conversation I couldn't determine if they were talking about the monumental battle in Belgium in 1944-45 or their dietary excesses.

I tactfully inserted myself into the conversation by ordering a round of Canadian Club and Seven-Up for all. I tossed a few quarters at the bartender, who archly thanked me for the tip and demanded I pay for the drinks. *A tempora, a mores!* Zenobia had gone bigtime in more ways than one.

Having had my wallet deflated by a significantly larger amount than I had anticipated, I asked my colleagues if any of them remembered Annie and, if so, where she was. Naturally, this triggered among the veterans an avalanche of sexual recollections, most of which were unsurprisingly similar: they had done it with Annie and had fond memories of her cheap rates and easy accessibility.

But was Annie still in town? Or even alive?

One of the less superannuated vets seemed to recall she had gone to an old folks' home near Hinesville. The others blearily agreed, thereby providing an endorsement that failed to fill me with confidence in my sources.

Still, a clue is a clue, and I decided to look into the situation. Sure enough, there was a Golden Days Retirement Village just south of Hinesville on U.S. 84, about halfway between Allenhurst and Fort Stewart. That figured. In her prime, Annie had turned tricks with soldiers and tourists she found at the truck stops and dives along that particularly notorious stretch of road. She probably made as much as the Long County sheriff used to off that rigged traffic light he operated in nearby Ludowici.

So Annie had returned to one of the scenes of her many triumphs. I took a chance and drove over.

She must have sensed my coming, for the relic who was now Pulpwood Annie was sitting in a wheelchair, staring at the parking lot as I pulled up. She immediately began to bounce up and down excitedly in the chair when she recognized me strolling up the walk.

"Can this be the infamous Pulpwood Annie?" I cautiously inquired.

"Can this be the smart-alecky college boy I used to baby-sit back in Zenobia?" she quickly rejoined.

Yes and yes.

Turned out that Annie's oft-used flesh had given out before her spirit did. A series of mini-strokes had incapacitated her several years back, and from her miniscule savings and heroic help from the Department of Child and Family Services, money for Annie was found within the cornucopia of federal funds earmarked for the indigent.

"I been livin' here for so long, I almost fergot what it was like to be out a-goin' and a-doin'," Annie confessed. "Can't complain, though. Got three squares a day and a bed that's a dern sight cleaner'n the one I had in my ol' trailer."

She began rattling on about some of the common names that had peppered the many stories she had told me. Most had died, reformed or entered the Grey Rock Hotel for an indeterminate time to serve before parole would be considered. She still had murderous feelings for the worthless LeRoy of "rubber popper" fame.

"Then I can assume you are happy and content with your new life of quiet and repose," I dared to venture.

"Phooey!" she replied with a shrill laugh. "Jes' ask them folks runnin' this dog house. I'm as much trouble as a boot full of barbed wire!"

I was glad to see she was still operating true to form, even if her method of mobilization was a wheelchair instead of her reliable old I-H pickup. We continued to chat for a while, but I soon sensed she was tiring. I chose the moment to break things off and retire.

"By the way, Annie, there's something I have been wanting to ask you for all these many years. Tried a dozen or more times, but something always interrupted my train of thought or distracted me until you had turned the corner with a customer."

"What you want to know?"

"Just this. Your last name. All these years, all I've ever known is Annie…Pulpwood Annie."

"Ain't that enough? Got you a whole lot of me ever time you said it out loud, didn't it?" She chuckled in recollection.

"Yeah, and more times when I didn't!"

"So what? It all washed out the same. We was supposed to spend some time together."

"Fortunately, my idea of 'together' stopped at the bedside even if yours didn't."

"Yeah, college boy, you missed out on a real ride. Sorry I can't accommodate you now."

"That's okay. Just tell me your last name."

Gray-haired and snaggle-toothed, her face a roadmap of wrinkles and wattles for which Maybelline was no longer the answer—if it ever had been—Annie squinted her familiar, red-rimmed eyes and studied me as she had many a time in the past. I knew the look: she was determining if I were ready for what she had to impart. As usual, I passed with flying colors.

"You're an over-educated jerk if you never figgered that one out," Annie said in a voice that brought back instant memories of our discourses at Bubba's. "You know all them pioneer wiregrass Georgia families married or bred into each other back when there wasn't a handful of white folks between Folkston and Macon. That includes your family and mine.

"My last name? Haw! Sonny boy, it's the same as yours!"

With that, she spun around in her wheelchair and streaked down the hallway. I could hear her cackling even as she made the turn.

Stunned by her unexpected revelation, I could only watch as she disappeared from sight. And that was the last time I ever saw the seemingly indescribable, indestructible, incandescent, unflappable, unforgettable and probably unsinkable Pulpwood Annie.

Printed in the United States
33441LVS00002B/73-78

9 781413 766998